When he went outside it was dark and there was no one around, except a man on the far side of the rutted street. Laskovy fiddled with the cinch straps of the horse as he eyed the stranger beneath the brim of his hat. The man seemed interested in him. Was he a bounty hunter?

As the man stepped into the street, Dan slid the Colt from his belt and cocked it. If it came to shooting, Rufe would be out of the door in a moment, backing him up.

He heard the stranger say, "Put your hands on the saddle where I can see 'em."

Instead, Dan turned and fired.

He saw the flash and smoke as the other pistol fired at the same time.

Also by Arthur Moore
Published by Fawcett Gold Medal Books:

TRAIL OF THE GATLINGS
THE KID FROM RINCON
STEEL BOX

DEAD
OR
ALIVE

Arthur Moore

FAWCETT GOLD MEDAL ● NEW YORK

Chapter One

IT was exactly 2:47 when Cory Durant tugged out the silver watch from his vest pocket and compared the time with the fancy gold and black clock across the street in the bank window. He was one minute slow or the bank was a minute fast. . . .

He clicked the lid closed and glanced along the street of front-flared buildings with their sagging porch overhangs, all with a beaten, long-settled look. Ruskin hadn't had a new building in five years. A few alleys ran back from the main drag, and the ornate orange and yellow windows of the saloon down the street were the only colors in the afternoon sun.

Three doors to the right a man was examining a wagon singletree, then pounding on it with a hammer. Horses stood three-footed at hitchracks, and a tiny vagrant breeze lifted a handful of dust that sparkled when the sun hit it. Two riders who looked like drifters came into the street and walked their horses past the wagon.

The riders got down in front of the bank, and Cory stretched out his legs, scratching his potbelly absently. Tilting the chair back, he chewed on a matchstick and watched the riders go up the steps into the bank's open door.

He had never seen either of the men before. The damned country was getting too populated since the stage line had come to town a year ago. There had been a time when a man knew everyone in the county.

Beside Cory were four empty chairs and a bench. The sun had left this side of the street, and the gabbers and spitters were all gathered in front of the hotel with its gingerbread cornices, five doors down from the bank. Cory yawned, then stared, catching sight of Phineas Erskine, the bank manager, as he passed the open door. Why the hell did Phineas have his hands up?

Cory blinked at the doorway. Just in front of it on the boardwalk was a two-sided sign that gave the bank's hours: 10 A.M. to 3 P.M. Cory let the chair down and bit his lip. Should he go across the street and look in the window? Phineas had certainly had his hands up. . . .

Then he saw one of the drifters look out to the street. It was a damned furtive look, Cory thought. He stared at the two horses at the hitchrack and rubbed his chin . . . and in that second heard the shot.

It came from inside. A cold hand grabbed Cory's vitals. Those two were robbing the bank! He jumped to his feet, mouth open, and could not decide what to do. Everything was whirling inside his head.

He sat down again abruptly as the two men came running from the bank, pistols in their hands. One wore a navy blue double-buttoned shirt, the other a checked shirt under a brown vest. They threw themselves onto the horses, and one fired a shot through the open doorway of the bank; then they were gone, galloping hell-bent for leather.

The sound of the shot jerked Cory out of the chair, and he began to run toward the marshal's office.

Rufe Wicker climbed on the bay horse and held the heavy money sack in front of him as he spurred the animal, pounding out of town with Dan close behind.

It had been as easy as he'd thought it would be. No bank in this end of the territory had been robbed in years, so they didn't expect it. Ruskin's marshal had no jurisdiction outside the town. They'd have to send to the sheriff for law, unless some of the hayseeds got together to form a posse.

They galloped past the stage depot and the lot, where several mud wagons waited, past the livery and the tar-paper shacks that straggled at the end of the street, and then they were in the open.

Rufe reined in to a lope and looked back. No one was following them. He grinned at Dan Laskovy. "Told you it'd be easy."

"Yeh." Dan's eyes were bright. "How much you figger we got?"

"We'll count it and divvy up tonight."

Around them were tawny meadows and a few worm fences. The road was well traveled. Out of sight of the town they turned off the road into a field, smelling the rank odor of a passing skunk. Behind them the dust hung in the air and drifted off lazily. A few torn bits of cloud curdled in the sky, and their shadows blurred the sun-baked earth and the sparse patches of bristling sage.

When they came to a dry wash that headed east, Rufe chuckled and kept the bay at a lope. He wanted to put distance between them and any trigger-happy bunch gathered up from the streets . . . not a likely thing.

The wash had a sandy bottom speckled with weeds and brown grass; their passing raised no dust. To the right the land stretched nearly flat, gray-brown, and marbled with low brush. To the right were scraggly trees and mesquite thickets, and in the sky a hawk slid down from high overhead, circling then diving to disappear in the distance.

He had picked Ruskin not only because it had not been robbed in years, but because there were few young men available in town to ride after them. And those few would take time to get organized, select a leader and equipment. It might be dark before they set out.

Rufe was a tallish, rangy man with prominent cheekbones and dark hair worn long. He was deeply tanned and had a beak of a nose and a black mustache. He wore a navy blue shirt and jeans that were nearly worn out, his only disguise. His name was Rufus, which he had always hated.

His mother had named him for a distant relative, or so they had told him. He had never known her.

He had been orphaned at the age of five and taken by a kindly preacher and put into the Baptist orphanage at Tullio, Oklahoma Territory, a dreary place at best. He had remained there till the age of fifteen when he'd slid out one night with several others and never looked back.

Climbing out of the wash, they made camp in a clutter of huge rocks, waiting for dark to make a tiny Indian fire so smoke would not be seen. Dan was the better cook. He set about making biscuits while Rufe cleaned the pistols.

Dan was short and sallow-faced. He had light, stringy hair, a sunburned face that did not tan readily, and little ears tight to his skull. He and Rufe had ridden together off and on for years. He was a man to guard your back, damned good with a gun . . . but a little quick to use it. One of the bankers had died because he reached under the counter. Another had hesitated a fraction of a second too long and been clouted with a pistol barrel; the man had fallen and twitched his life away.

A third man had been hit and knocked ass over teakettle. They had stepped over him on the way out.

Rufe would have preferred that no shots be fired at all because the noise could be heard on the street. Someone might oppose them as they ran for the horses.

But no one had. An older man, sitting across the street, had started to run along the boardwalk, but Rufe had ignored him.

There was eighteen thousand dollars in the two sacks they carried. Rufe had hoped for more—was there ever enough? They divided the loot evenly and agreed to hang together for mutual protection till they reached Oklahoma. Not a far piece.

Dan had decided to see New Orleans before they'd gone on the job, but now he was of two minds. There was a gal in Pueblo . . . and since he was in tall cotton, he might just go and swing on her gate.

Rufe thought he would go down into Texas. His wife

was staying at their ranch near Saylor, and he hadn't seen her in two months.

John Fleming, Chief of Security Operations, West, was a large, paunchy man who was almost never seen without a cigar. His clothes were constantly dusted with ashes, his sleeves had burn holes, and his office smelled of tobacco. His coworkers said everyone in Washington, D.C., could smell him.

He pushed papers across the desk to Laredo. "Here's what we know about Rufus Wicker. We're certain he was one of the two men who robbed the bank in Ruskin and killed three people."

"Why are you sure?"

"One called the other 'Rufe.' How many do you know named Rufus? Besides, he matches the description; so does Laskovy. The second man was probably Dan Laskovy. We know he's been running with Wicker."

Laredo scanned the reports and handed them to Pete Torres. "One man shot and two hit with revolver barrels, according to the witnesses. One man died two days after the robbery."

Laredo was a big man with tawny blond hair and regular, rather square features with dark eyes and a solid jaw. His dark suit strained and stretched over the shoulders. He and Pete were members of the elite Bluestar unit of the Tanner Detective Organization.

Pete Torres was slightly larger than Laredo, dark, with black eyes and hair. He had a quick mind and excelled with a rifle under any circumstances.

Fleming said, "Wicker is very high on our wanted list. He and Laskovy are very dangerous. We estimate they've killed about twenty men between them, give or take a few. Witnesses at the bank say Laskovy accounted for all three deaths. He is quick as a sidewinder."

Laredo took the papers back and frowned at them.

Fleming dumped ashes into a huge receptable. "There's talk that Rufe has a ranch somewhere in Texas. If so, he may head for it. Maybe both of them will. But they've got

5

money now, so they may not. It's not easy to outguess outlaws in that regard."

Pete asked, "Have they been seen since they left Ruskin?"

"Yes, in Oklahoma Territory. That's why we think they may be heading for Texas."

Laredo glanced up. "It says here Wicker has connections with the Porter gang—train robbers."

Fleming nodded. "I was about to mention that." He puffed smoke. "Are you taking the job?"

"Exactly what is the job?"

Fleming looked at the end of the cigar. "We want Rufe Wicker and Dan Laskovy dead or alive. How's that for clarity?"

"Not bad." Laredo smiled. "Gives us a clue."

Chapter Two

THE town marshal's office in Ruskin was on a side street. In the small square room were several rawhide straight-back chairs, a Seth Thomas clock with thin black hands, a rifle rack with only two Winchesters pointing at the ceiling, a long-suffering desk, and a clutter of posters on the walls.

The marshal was named Emory Spooner, according to the sign on the door in yellow letters. He wore a rusty black suit and was weathered gray as a horned toad. He was about to lock up for the day when they arrived.

It was getting dark, and he paused with an unlit lantern in his hand. "Howdy, gents . . ."

Laredo showed his credentials. "We're here about the robbery and murders."

The marshal put the lantern down. "You-all's federals?"

"We work for the federal government on contract." Laredo waited while the other man put on his specs and studied the credentials.

"Nobody told me you was coming." He indicated the door, and they filed inside and he closed it. "What you want to know?"

"Anything you can tell us. We are specifically after Wicker and Laskovy."

The marshal nodded. "That Lassovy, he kilt the three of them. Course you know that trail's a week old. . . ."

7

"Yes," Pete said. "Did you form a posse and go after them?"

Spooner shook his head. He took off his hat and laid it on the desk. "No—we didn't. Not for about a day, till we could get us some men together. Damn trail petered out anyways. And there ain't no trackers around, not like they used to be. Guess they all workin' for the cavalry."

"Tell us what you can," Laredo directed him.

"Well, they come into the bank 'bout a quarter to three, fifteen minutes b'fore closing. Cory Durant, he was sittin' across the street, and he looked at his watch 'bout that time. They was two of 'em, and they told Phineas, he's the bank manager, to open the safe. Phineas said it was already open."

"So they filled some sacks?"

"That's right. Two sacks."

Pete asked, "How many in the bank?"

"Lessee—Phineas, Jack Hubbard, Buford Waters, Eli Cramm, and Viola Matthews. Five. Jack was the one shot, and Eli and Buford was hit. Buford died in the bank, but Eli held on till the next day." Spooner shook his head sadly. "We never had us a mass funeral b'fore."

"What about the woman?"

"Viola is a bookkeeper. She a woman about fifty. They told her to sit, and she did. They never touched her."

Laredo asked, "How long were they in the bank?"

"Not very long. They had the sacks with 'em. Shoved the money in the sacks and run out. Phineas says Eli and Buford was slow. Jack was reaching for something when Lassovy shot him."

"The two men were identified from pictures?"

"Yes. No doubt 'bout that. You ain't talked to nobody else yet?"

"Not yet."

It was all the marshal knew. They thanked him and went around to the hotel, the only one in town. It had long since gone to seed, but it had a billiard parlor on one side and a barroom on the other. They read the weekly in the lobby and went upstairs to bed.

In the morning they had breakfast, then walked to the

bank and talked to Phineas Erskine. He was a skinny man of about sixty years, wearing thick glasses. He was very pale, with caved-in cheeks and a big Adam's apple. He could easily have been an alderman in a church.

He told them the bank had been closed for three days after the robbery. The sheriff had sent a deputy to ask him questions and had taken a lot of notes, but nothing had happened. "We're getting back to normal now—not quite as we were, but we'll be adequate until the new people learn their jobs."

Laredo asked, "Did you offer a reward?"

"Yes, two thousand dollars. It was a terrible thing, gentlemen, a really terrible thing! I have never been that close to such violence before."

He had few other details to add to those of the marshal, and the identities of the robbers were undoubted.

Viola Matthews said, "I heard one call the other 'Rufe.' They put me in a room and told me to stay there. I got a very good look at both of them."

She had picked their photographs out of fifteen or more. She was very definite.

They found Cory Durant in his accustomed place, in a tilted-back chair opposite the bank. Evidently that was his occupation. He was retired from the railroad, he told them, and his wife had gone a few years back. He had nothing else to do. Yes, he had seen the two riders get down in front of the bank at precisely 2:49. His watch had not varied in thirty years, but the bank clock was a minute fast. He had seen Phineas Erskine pass the open door with his hands in the air. He had thought that odd—and then he had heard the shot from inside and knew the bank was being robbed.

"One of 'em fired into the open door of the bank as they got on the horses," Durant said. "Then they was gone." He pointed south along the street.

"Why didn't the marshal go after them?"

"Well, they was only half a dozen young fellers in town, and only one of them had a gun and a horse. Old folks like me, we wasn't about to go chasin' killers."

Laredo thanked the man, and they went back to the

hotel lobby. Laredo then asked his partner, "Where did they go?"

"Back to Texas. Fleming says Rufe's got a ranch down there . . . somewhere."

"He's also got a lot of money in his kick. Will they save it or spend it?"

Pete shrugged. "What do we know about them—have they got a record of saving money?"

"No. They're both hold-up men by trade. Spend it soon's they get it. What's your vote . . . do we go to Texas?"

Pete nodded. "It's our best bet."

Dan Laskovy decided to go to Pueblo. He and Rufus would keep track of each other by mail. In Nevis there was a saloon run by a friend who would keep or forward letters for them.

When he and Rufe stopped over at Gurley Bend, he bought a small suitcase, a suit like drummers wore, a pair of plain-glass specs, and a soft hat. Dressed in this disguise, he paraded for Rufe, who swore no one would recognize him in that getup.

At Gurley Bend Rufe and Dan had bought all the newspapers and read the accounts of the deed at Ruskin. Three had died instead of two. Too bad. The bank manager's account of the amount stolen was correct. The latest paper said the trail had been lost.

No newspaper mentioned the Tanner Organization or its agents. And all accounts said the bank had been entered by two men, Rufus Wicker and Dan Laskovy. Identification had been positive.

Rufe growled, "How the hell they so damn sure?"

"They got pictures."

Rufe had been photographed by the law when he'd been arrested in Arizona several years before. Dan had been photographed in the territorial prison where he served three years. Obviously the pictures had been distributed to county sheriffs everywhere on wanted sheets and posters.

Laskovy then sold his horse and saddle and took the stage the next day.

Rufe continued on south.

He looked like a drifter; the sack with the money was tied on with his blanket roll as a food sack or warbag. There was no reason anyone would give it a second glance.

It took Rufe two weeks to ride to Saylor, a small, sleepy town in west Texas. He did not enter the town but circled it and rode on to his ranch, five miles farther. Thelma shouted and ran out to him as he stepped down.

He had married Thelma in Denver several years past, when he'd been in the chips. Ranch women were often shapeless, usually bonneted and tough as boot leather. Thelma was anything but that. She had been working in a house but had left the life and promised to settle down and devote herself only to him. So far she had.

It had been fun, traveling from place to place, to Kansas City and St. Louis, in fancy suites, eating in the best restaurants, buying her clothes . . . until the money ran out.

Thelma had stayed in the hotel then, and Rufe had gone out to ply his trade. He had lifted near six hundred dollars from unwary travelers, and the two of them had hurried back to Texas.

A stage holdup on the way had netted them enough to buy the ranch near Saylor.

Thelma had fixed the house up with calico curtains and a turkey rug, some harp-legged furniture and mirrors, a few pictures on the walls, and Rufe felt very comfortable. It was as fine as many of the line houses he'd been in. There was even a cut-glass chandelier.

He'd been happy there for half a year, until the itch got at him and he'd written to Dan Laskovy. They were getting low on cash. Thelma understood the itch.

He met Dan in Gurley Bend, and they headed north, seeking a likely prospect. Ruskin happened to be a town in their path. They cased the bank for several days, then rode in one afternoon and took it, expecting more, but eighteen thousand was not spoiled turnips.

Nine thousand each was no small amount. In Gurley Bend they had seen some old wanted posters. They were

11

each worth eight hundred to a bounty hunter. But after Ruskin it would go up, sure as a gun.

Thelma had been delighted to see him back so soon. She insisted he take a bath before he crawled into bed; he grumbled, but she poured the water for him and washed him as he sat in the round metal tub. She asked, "How much did you get?"

"We divvied up eighteen thousand. Even up."

"Jeez, Rufe . . . we can go to New Orleans. You wanted to go, remember?"

"Sure." He stood, and she rinsed him off and dried him. After a while they ate, finished a bottle and slept very late the next morning. Then he let her count the money and stack it on a table to gaze at.

The ranch consisted of sixty acres, most given over to brush and weeds. Thelma had made a small vegetable garden; there were two milk cows, a half-dozen chickens for eggs, and a goat. There was a large shed for the mule and a buckboard. She seldom went into the barn.

She had been going into town once or twice a month, or whenever the lonelies became too pressing. There she would give the grocer her list, then go on to the back rooms of the Nugget or the Golden Horn and smoke a cigar and gab with the girls for a few hours.

After that she would pick up the supplies from the store and drive home to the same empty house.

Occasionally a rider came by, usually some hand looking for the road to town, and she would feed him for the conversation, or give him a drink—but she was true to Rufe, in most cases.

Rufe was worn out from the long weary ride; he wasn't getting any younger, he said. Each winter was harder than the last. When he talked seriously to her, he would say he ought to be thinking of one or two big scores, then quit. It would be nice to settle somewhere he wasn't known, to save their money instead of throwing it to the winds, and have no worries about the county sheriff.

Wasn't that possible? Thelma encouraged him in the idea.

He spent hours sleeping each day, and when he woke,

she would fix him a fine breakfast, and they often sat on the gallery talking about New Orleans. Rufe thought they could cross Texas by stagecoach, then find their way to Natchez or another of the river towns and go down the Mississippi by steamboat. He had heard about those steamboats and wanted to see one and ride on one.

A week after he arrived Thelma went into town with the buckboard to pick up supplies and see if there was any mail. Rufe saddled his horse and accompanied her partway; he did not enter the town. There was no sense in advertising his presence. Probably half the town knew him by sight, and if there were any of those damned wanted posters about he would cause talk.

The kind of talk a bounty hunter liked to hear. Eight hundred dollars, dead or alive, was a hell of a lot of money to some back-shooter. Rufe did not intend to provide that kind of windfall.

Thelma gave the grocer her usual list and went on to the Nugget to smoke a quick cigar and gab for a bit. Rufe would not approve, but she did not tell him everything. . . .

She listened to the latest saloon gossip, without mentioning Rufe, and went back to the store for her staples. There was no mail.

He was waiting for her outside the town. He tied the horse on behind the buckboard, and they returned home together. He asked immediately, "Did you hear any news?"

She looked at him and made a face. "Only one thing you'd be interested in . . ."

"Yeh? What's that?"

"You're worth more."

"What?"

"The reward for you and Dan has been increased."

His brows lifted. "Izzat so? What am I worth?"

"One thousand dollars, dead or alive."

Rufe whistled.

13

Chapter Three

THE wanted sheet told them that Rufus Wicker had spent time in the Texas town of Longworth. He'd had a relative there who had since died. Laredo thought it worthwhile to look at the town. Anything they could learn about Wicker would be valuable.

They went across country, avoiding distant cabins and peeled log houses; they saw a distant rider now and then, and when they came across a road going in their direction, they followed it. A freighter with four mules nodding stopped, and the driver yelled, asking for news.

"Been up in the damn hills for a week talkin' to these here ginger mules."

Laredo told the man what he knew, and the wagon rolled on past with a rattle of cable chains. They saw no one else for a day, slept in a notch of coulee at night, and the next day about noon they came in sight of a town as a light rain began to fall.

The town proved to be Lichfield, a dozen miles from Longworth, but they decided to stay the night and sleep in a bed. Lichfield, named after the oldest inhabitant, was a cow town that went to sleep Monday and did not awaken till the following Saturday. Most of the houses were raw-timbered and shabby with weather. The few stores along the wide rutted street had board awnings, and the boardwalk did not travel the length of the town but stopped and

14

started again with rickety steps down to the hitchracks and a couple of troughs.

The only hotel had a lobby the size of a watch pocket, with a squeezed-in desk and narrow steps to the second floor. Half the space was taken up by a black stove. There was a string stretched across it, and a shirt and pair of jeans were hung on the string to dry.

"Fifty cents for the night, gents," an old man told them. "You got your own blankets? Stable an' privies out back."

Their first move was to call on the deputy sheriff assigned to the town. His name, so the sign on the door told them, was Homer Cross. He proved to be a lean, sour-faced man with black hair and bony hands who examined their credentials with turned-down mouth and handed them back.

"What you fellers want?"

Laredo said pleasantly, "We're mainly looking for Rufus Wicker. Anything you can do to—"

"Ever'body's looking for Wicker. Nothing I can tell you."

Pete said, "We're told he used to hang out here."

The deputy seemed to bristle. "I don't allow criminals to hang out in my town." He scowled at them. "And we don't need no fed'ral officers. Why don't you-all just clear out?"

Laredo smiled. "Do we get twenty-four hours to hit the trail, Mr. Cross?"

"Something like that."

"We aren't allowed to stay in your town? Are you calling us criminals?"

Cross looked from one to the other. "I ain't calling you nothing. I said you ain't needed here."

"And you have no information for us . . ."

"Not a thing."

Laredo smiled again. "From one lawman to another, you're not very cooperative. You wouldn't be protecting Rufe Wicker, would you?"

"Why, you goddam—!" The deputy rushed at Laredo, long arms flailing. Laredo stepped aside, and his open

15

hand caught the lean man under the chin, snapping his head back. A knee in the stomach doubled the man up, and the deputy was suddenly sitting on the floor looking dazed.

Pete heaved the man up and dropped him into a chair. Cross slumped, head on his chin, taking deep breaths. Then he suddenly faced around with a pistol in his hand. Pete was behind him, waiting for such a move. A quick chop hit the deputy's wrist, and the pistol clattered across the board floor to thump against the wall. Laredo picked it up and unloaded it without a word.

Cross held his hurt wrist, glowering. "You two get the hell outa my town—hear?"

Laredo crossed and sat on the edge of the desk, looking down at the deputy. "No, Mr. Cross, we will not. We never look for trouble, but I assure you we can be more trouble than you'd care to tackle . . . if it comes to that." He laid the revolver on the desk.

Cross said nothing as they left the office and closed the door. Laredo sighed. "Very disappointing."

"I think he knows things he's not willing to tell us."

"Yes. We can ask around and see what we scare up."

"One thing," Pete said.

"What?"

"Now we're in the middle between the crooks and the law."

Laredo grinned. "An interesting place to be."

The day clerk at the hotel was a young man, skinny and pop-eyed behind his steel-rimmed glasses. He wore a striped shirt with blue armbands because the sleeves were too long. He was studying, he told them, to go to college at Austin to become a lawyer.

"Too many lawyers now," Pete said.

The lad scratched his jaw with a pen holder. "I *was* considering land."

"Land?"

"Yes. The Townsite Act of 1844 provides that a group can stake out three-hundred-twenty acres, divide the land into lots, and sell them."

16

"Why not do that?" Laredo asked.

"Well, there was an amendment. You have to have one hundred persons in the group to qualify because of land speculation. I finally decided it was too risky."

"So you're going to law school . . ."

The lad nodded and grinned. "It beats working."

Pete asked, "Did you ever hear of Rufe Wicker?"

"Yes, sure. I read about him in the papers. He robs banks, doesn't he?"

"Yes, and kills people. Did you ever see him here, in town?"

The lad shook his head. "I don't think so . . ."

Laredo said, "If you think of anything about him, we'd like to know."

"All right. My name's Gordon, by the way."

They shook hands with him, then went to supper.

In the first saloon, the Two Barrels, the barman shook his head. "Don't know any Wicker." He moved away, shaking his head. Pete tossed a coin on the bar, and he came back looking surly. "Don't know anything about him."

"Did he hang out here in town?"

The man shook his head again, making a sour face. "I don't know."

In the second saloon the lone bartender was more friendly. He was reading a newspaper when they entered; the room was nearly deserted. Pete ordered beer for Laredo and himself.

At the question, did he know Wicker, the bartender put down the paper. "You-all lawmen?"

Laredo admitted they were. "What about Wicker?"

"Well, he's been in here, but I ain't seen him for a long time, more'n half a year at least. What's the reward on him now?"

"It just went up to a thousand."

"Jesus!" The bartender whistled. "Sure like to collect that!" He drew the two beers and shoved them across the bar. "I'd leave the old woman and head west."

17

Laredo asked, "You got any idea where we can find Rufe?"

The barman sighed. "No. I dunno anybody he was tight with. Talk is, he's a loner."

They finished the beer, thanked the man, and went out. Wicker left damned few tracks behind. It was like chasing a shadow.

There were six men sitting in the third saloon, most smoking and gossiping. They looked the newcomers over and went on with their discussion. The bartender told them he had read something about Wicker but had never seen him.

None of the gossipers seemed eager to help either. They only shook their heads dumbly when Laredo asked them, and stared back at him.

In the street in front of the saloon Pete rolled a cigarette and looked at the sky. "A lot of nowhere, *amigo*." He scratched a match. "The man's a killer. He can't have many friends."

"They're afraid of him."

"I suppose . . ."

A seedy-looking man came from the saloon, looked at Pete's cigarette, and asked if he could spare a smoke. Pete handed him a Bible and a sack of Durham, and they watched him roll a smoke very unsteadily. The man looked up at them from under shaggy brows. "Heard you was askin' about Rufe Wicker."

"That's right. Did you know him?"

The man puffed, looked at the cigarette, and nodded. "But he ain't been in town here for a right good spell, not that I seen, anyways."

"Do you know where we might find him?"

"Saylor."

"Saylor? What's that?"

The other puffed hard, then tossed the messy cigarette away in disgust. "It's a town south of here. Heard Rufe say one night he had a ranch near there. He was a little drunk, I guess."

Pete smiled, dug in a pocket, and handed the man a dollar. "Buy yourself some smokes, friend."

"Thanks."

According to the map they consulted, Saylor was a small burg some eighty miles south as the crow flew. It was a long way from nowhere, the kind of place to suit an owlhoot like Wicker just fine. He would need a place to hole up in, a safe haven between jobs. They wondered if his wife was there. Probably.

Chapter Four

SAYLOR was a sorry little wide place in the trail with weather-beaten houses and ramshackle stores on one side of the street only. Weeds grew everywhere, even in the wheel ruts. There were a few corrals on the opposite side of the street where dust rose with every breeze. As they rode in, the town had a strong smell to it, the wind not interested enough in chasing it out.

The only saloon was a deadfall called by the owner's name, Hadden's Place. It had a dirt floor and boards set on barrels for a bar. Hadden was behind the bar, an unshaven, shifty-eyed man who told them he had never heard of anyone named Wicker.

"Nobody by that name in this here county."

When they went out to the street again, Pete said, "I wouldn't trust him to tell me the day of the week, but in that case I think he was telling the truth."

"That's kind of involved reasoning . . ."

"I s'pose it is. Let's try the store."

The general store was small and cluttered. There was barely room to walk in and edge to the back counter. It was run by an old man who was hard of hearing and could not understand their questions. Pete finally wrote out: Do you know Rufe Wicker?

The old man shook his head, and they went out to the street. The town had no hotel and no law, but it had a blacksmith shop next to the grocery. The blacksmith was a middle-aged man wearing a leather apron and a bowler hat. He had heard of Wicker but didn't think anyone in the county had that name.

Laredo had an idea. "What about a woman living alone?"

"Yes—there's Miz Henderson. And Miz Wilson—she lives out of town. Comes in a few times a month. Had to fix her buckboard las' year."

"Wilson," Laredo said, glancing at Pete. "We may have the name wrong. It could be Wilson, not Wicker."

"Not a bad-lookin' woman," the blacksmith said. "Says her man is up north some'eres on business. I ain't never seen him."

"Where's the Wilson place?"

The blacksmith stepped into the street and pointed. "You foller this road 'bout four, five mile. It kind of peters out, but you can see wagon tracks. Nobody uses it much but Miz Wilson. Anyway, you come to a sandhill, and just beyond it you see trees off to the left. That's where the house is."

"Thanks."

It was late in the afternoon. They went back to the deadfall and ordered beer. If Rufe was at the house, it would not be a smart idea to ride up in daylight. Although they didn't know the lay of the land, they would have to approach the house at night . . . and hope there were no half-wild dogs to greet them.

The trail was as the blacksmith had said, barely visible on the ground and lost altogether on hard-packed earth. They reached the sandhill before dark and dismounted to wait. Beyond the hill were distant trees.

An hour after dark they mounted again and walked the horses toward the trees. They were on a level plain where dark brush picked at them. The trees proved to be dusty cottonwoods.

They went single file, in no hurry, and the wood petered out in less than half a mile. As they sat the horses at the edge of it, they could make out the dark silhouettes of

21

several buildings not far off. One of them had lit windows.

"Maybe we can see in," Laredo said softly. "Could be Rufe is sitting by the fire."

Pete made a rude sound. "And maybe Christmas will come in October."

"You have a skeptical streak . . ."

"Call it reality instead. If Rufe is in that house, he is not likely to sit near an open window."

"If he's home, he ought to consider himself safe . . . isn't it possible?"

Pete shrugged. "It's possible."

They tied the horses and went on slowly, listening and watchful, being very careful where they stepped; sounds carried far in the stillness. There were no fences at all, and as they came close to the house it was apparent the windows were heavily curtained. It would be impossible to see in. Laredo swore under his breath.

They conferred in whispers. "If he's in there, what'll he do if we pound on the door?"

"Go out a window," Pete said promptly.

"We can't watch all four sides of the house."

"Then don't pound on the door."

Laredo sighed. "Try to be some help, *amigo*."

"All right. Then let's set fire to the barn. That ought to get him out."

"Won't he wonder how the fire started? It'll alert him."

"Anything we do will alert him," Pete said reasonably. "This *hombre* is an outlaw."

Laredo frowned. That was true. Probably a change in the weather would alert Rufe. He had spent his life on the alert. So why not set fire to the barn? "Let's do it," he said.

They went back and circled the barn. It was not a large structure and rather shacky, a hundred yards from the house. There were two mules inside, and Pete led them out. Pete found a can of coal oil, tracking it down by smell, and splashed it over a pile of dry straw.

Laredo scratched a match and tossed it onto the straw.

It was astonishing how fast the fire licked up the wall of the barn. They ran out and hurried toward the house, hearing the crackle of the greedy flames becoming louder and louder.

The fire burst out of a barn window, shooting sparks high into the air. A second later someone emptied a six-gun in their general direction. Laredo hit the dirt—the fire was making the yard as bright as day!

Rufe was alert as hell, Laredo thought. Undoubtedly years of ducking the law had given him another pair of eyes in the back of his head, and a sixth sense concerning lawmen.

Laredo lay behind a low shed out of sight of anyone in the house. Pete was off to his left somewhere. Glancing back, he could see the barn going up like a rocket. It must be dry as gunpowder; sparks were spilling into the dark sky, twinkling prettily. He could feel the warmth of the fire and hear the crackling heart of it . . . and then he heard something else! Hoofbeats!

Jumping up, Laredo ran toward the back of the house. He drew fire. Someone was shooting at him from a house window, but the shots went wild. At the rear of the house he halted, swearing. Rufe had gotten away! He'd had a horse saddled and ready . . . just in case.

Pete came trotting from the far side of the house. "He got away—?"

Laredo nodded, blowing out his breath in annoyance. "He had a horse saddled and waiting—and he knows this country." It would take them five minutes or so to run back for their horses, and by that time Rufe would be gone.

"Who was that shooting?"

"His wife tried to keep us occupied." Laredo studied the burning barn. It was nearly consumed, falling in on itself. They had flushed out Rufe all right.

Pete said, "Aiding and abetting. We can put her in the carcel for that."

"What good?"

"Rufe might try to get her out, and we'd be waiting."

Laredo sighed deeply. "Maybe . . . but I doubt it. He knows we wouldn't hold her for long. No jury in Texas is going to jail her for helping her man."

Pete grunted. "You're telling me a bullet fired by a woman won't kill anyone."

"Right. That's what I'm saying."

"You belong on that jury."

Laredo sighed again, and they went back for the horses.

They returned to the Wicker house in the morning. There proved to be a trail around the sandhill, cutting through the low brush, where meadowlarks were singing. As they rode into the trees they could smell the burned ashes of the barn.

When the house came into view, they saw it was a modest frame building with a shake roof. Someone had put a coat of red paint on the boards, probably when it had been built, and it had glass in the windows they could see. There was a gallery or porch on one side with three or four chairs scattered along it. A half-dozen cottonwoods shaded it, the leaves flickering green and gray.

The barn site was a blackened pile. The fire had taken several sheds with it, and a tall woman was in among the ashes with a hoe. She wore a brown calico dress with long sleeves and a high neck. She turned and shaded her eyes when she heard the horses.

Laredo approached her and touched his hat brim. "You Miz Wicker, ma'am?"

She studied them both, and her voice was steely. "My name is Wilson. What do you want?"

"We're looking for Rufe."

She shook her head. "Nobody by that name here."

Pete asked, "You live here alone, ma'am?"

"That's none of your business."

"I see you had a fire," Laredo said innocently. He leaned on the horn and looked about him as she glared. "You wouldn't have any idea where we could locate Rufe?"

"I don't think you're friends of his."

Pete asked, "You know all his friends?"

She scowled at him, seemed to hesitate in answering, then said, "I know a lot of 'em."

24

"So your name *is* Wicker." Laredo gave her a wide smile.

She shook the hoe at him. "You-all get off my land! You hear! I got nothing to say to you!"

Nudging the bay horse, Laredo rode around her to the back of the house. Rufe's tracks were plain on the ground; he had headed north in a big hurry. He glanced back at Mrs. Wicker. She still stood in the midst of the blackened barn site, lips compressed, clutching the hoe. He touched his hat again and turned away.

Laredo and Pete followed the tracks for a mile or more till the markings joined a cattle track. The tracks were still evident for another few miles, then joined a well-beaten trail that ran from the southeast to the northwest. Rufe's horse tracks mingled with a thousand others, and Laredo shook his head, reining in.

Pete said, "He left in a hurry—probably took nothing with him."

"Unless he had a warbag on the horse."

"Is he going to clear out of this part of the country—or will he hang close?"

Laredo stood in the stirrups and peered around them. "How much time do I have to answer that?"

"Take all day," Pete said. "It's an important question."

"Well, for the moment I vote we go back to talk to Deputy Cross while we think about it. Maybe he'll have changed his mind."

Pete snorted. "And maybe the moon will fall out of the sky."

Chapter Five

THEY went first to Saylor and talked to their friend the blacksmith. There was a railroad at Hartwell, only about forty miles distant, he told them. "We gets all our goods from there."

If a man were interested in fast transportation to some other place, Hartwell was the spot. Would Rufe Wicker see it that way?

Pete thought he would.

They bought some airtights at the general store and took the horses to a trough for water.

Laredo said, "But he only saw his wife a few days. Would he go off and leave her again?"

"It's guesswork either way. And what about Laskovy? He wasn't with Wicker at the house. That means they separated after the Ruskin job."

Laredo dug out a coin. "Heads we go to Hartwell, tails we watch the house. That all right?"

Pete nodded, and Laredo flipped the coin. It came down heads.

They rode across the prairie turf with a sigh of breeze close overhead. The horizons were empty, and the dust of the morning hung high in the air. They would reach Hartwell if they went southwest, and the town would be hard to miss because of the rails.

When they reached the railroad tracks, they would have to guess which way the town lay, unless they were near enough to see smoke.

The skies became duller as clouds drifted from the west, and toward evening rain threatened. Cloud shadows lowered, and the prairie stirred, moving in subtle fashion as if it breathed. But it did not rain, and they came to the shining steel rails at dusk.

"I vote we make camp," Laredo said. "The town could be twenty miles from here."

"Don't see any lights," Pete said, stretching his neck.

They got out dried beef and broiled it, heated some beans, and made coffee. They ate the beans with crackers, and Pete rolled a smoke as they sipped the coffee. The clouds wandered off to the east, and cold, crisp stars appeared, hanging just out of reach.

In the morning they found the town only a mile away, close by a ridge of low hills. It straggled along the tracks and boasted several trees by the station, which was in the center of town beside the square.

The station was painted a dull green color with black trim. The name Hartwell had been lettered on the end of the building. They got down and looked at the train schedule tacked on the wall beside the waiting room door. There had been a train four days ago, heading east. The next one was two days away.

The next train west was five days away.

Pete said, "They don't do a land-office business from this stop."

The stationmaster confirmed that observation. He was a skinny oldster with thick spectacles and false teeth that clacked a bit as he talked. "We don't get hardly any passengers, but there's freight. Wouldn't stop here at all if it wasn't for the freight."

Laredo showed him a wanted poster of Wicker. "Have you seen this man?"

The old man pushed his hat back and blinked at the paper. Pete said, "We think he may have taken the train from here a few days ago."

"Don't think so . . ."

"Why not?"

"Nobody but Miz Emily got on the train four days ago. She going to visit her kinfolk in Kansas City. Nobody got on the westbound. . . ."

"Could he have gotten on the train and you didn't know it?"

The old man nodded. "But the conductor woulda found 'im . . . put 'im off at the next stop." He grinned at them. "But he didn't."

"How d'you know that?"

"Cause I'm the telegrapher, and I'm talking up and down the line ever' day. I woulda heard." The old man nodded to them and went into his office.

They sat in the tiny waiting room, and Pete rolled a smoke. "We've lost 'im. If he didn't come here, God knows where he went."

It was discouraging.

Laredo sent a wire to John Fleming in their code, telling him of the events up to Hartwell. He suggested in the wire that they backtrack and perhaps pick up something they had missed.

In his return wire Fleming agreed that was a good idea. He also said he was sending a photograph of Rufe taken with two members of the Porter gang when they were celebrating something or other in St. Joseph. It was the best photo he had seen of Wicker; he would send it to Hartwell.

It would probably take a week to arrive.

Hartwell was a cow town. It shipped cattle east. It was also a commercial center with several warehouses that supplied dozens of stores scattered throughout the area. Wagons and wains were constantly coming and going. The large herds came twice a year, filling the corrals along the tracks, though smaller bunches were shipped during the year at odd times.

The largest hotel was the Drover's Rest on the main drag. It was a two-story edifice with gingerbread trim along the front, painted white, two heavy double doors, and a square lobby with a dozen bulky chairs and sofas.

It was a slow time, and they were able to get a single room with two beds. It also had two water pitchers and granite basins on washstands, a corner wardrobe, and some faded chromos of landscapes on the walls. The single window had yellowed lace curtains, and there were a dozen week-old flowers in a green vase on the windowsill.

The restaurant next door served them on white enameled plates and in heavy coffee mugs. The food was adequate, the town was half-asleep, and the weather warmed.

It took forever for the westbound to puff into the station. When the express mail was sorted, there was a brown envelope for them. It contained three copies of the photograph Fleming had mentioned. Rufe Wicker stared at them in company with two other hard cases, all heavily armed.

On the backs of the photos the two were identified as Harvey Elland and George Docker, alias Kid Dock. Both of the Porter Gang, train robbers.

The next morning they rolled their blankets, paid the bill, and rode out, heading north.

Rufe was astonished and alarmed when the fire in the barn became evident. Was the house surrounded? He ran to the back as Thelma emptied a revolver from a front window, firing blindly.

His buckskin was still saddled and waiting—that meant they hadn't gotten to the back yet or they'd have led the horse away at once. He kissed Thelma quickly. "I'll get word t'you soon's I can—" and ran out as she fired the rifle through a side window.

He got clean away; no shots followed him.

He had no doubts the law had set the fire—a deputy or maybe a bounty hunter wanting to flush him out. He was worth a thousand dollars now. And if they got him into a courtroom, he would hang. They had enough to hang him half a dozen times.

How the hell had they found him in Saylor? He growled about it as he hit the northwest trail. He would go to Peevy's place and lay up. It wasn't as satisfactory as sleeping with his own wife, but it was quiet and safe. No one

29

but Dan Laskovy knew about Peevy and the log-and-stone house in the hills, only a day's ride to Longworth.

Peevy was getting along in years now, but he had been a wild kid who'd grown up in the pear thickets of the Brasada and had made a sometime living signing saloon checks with his six-gun till somebody with a Winchester had busted his leg all to hell and stove him up for a year. Now he could only get about on a wooden peg and had to sell his saddle and ride a buckboard to go anywhere.

He pointed east and came across a wide cattle trail and followed it northeast for several days, passing several double-trailed wagons pulled by oxen and a third wagon loaded with buffalo bones and horns.

He turned off the trail by guess and went across country watching for smoke. When he saw it, he got down and waited. At dusk he rode close to the town, making sure it was Longworth. Some of the land south of the town was fenced with rails laid worm fashion, cross-staked and ridered. He rode past the fences and toward the distant low hills. When he reached them, he reined in and unsaddled the buckskin.

It wouldn't do to yell to Peevy at night. He would probably answer with rifle lead. He'd been owlhooting too long to get out of the habit.

Rufe rolled in his blankets and let the dawn come stealing in like an Apache.

In the morning he saddled the horse, warmed the bit for a moment in his gloves before slipping it into the buckskin's mouth, and continued on his way to the house. It had changed hardly at all except for the corral close to the side door where two brown mules stared at him indifferently and a gray cat looked him over from the top rail.

When he yelled for Peevy, the cat took off in a gray streak. Peevy came to the door with a shotgun under his arm. He peered out, bending forward, screwing up his face.

"Who the hell's that?"

"It's me, you old good for nothing."

Peevy grunted. "Shiiiit, it's Rufus. The law after you agin, Rufe?"

"Goddam law's allus after me." Rufe opened the corral gate and put the horse inside. "You-all want some company?" He went up the steps to the door.

Peevy looked exactly as he had a year ago. The same weathered, lined face, thick glasses, and gimpy leg, all wood from the knee down. Peevy stumped inside and shut the door after Rufe.

"Find a place'n sit. You rid far?"

"Came from down in Texas. Can you keep me for a week or so? I got money."

"Hell, yes. Keep you for a month if you want. What'd you do this time?"

"Me'n Dan, we robbed us a bank over to Ruskin. You know where that is?"

"No."

"Over the other end of the terr'tory. Got away with only a couple thousand. We hit the bank at the wrong time, I reckon." He looked around the cluttered room. It smelled a little gamy, but Peevy always smelled that way. He probably hadn't had a bath since Grant took Richmond.

Peevy found a bottle and dusted it off. "Got some rectified whiskey. Had me some Mormon, but it weren't aged long enough to kill whatever went into it." He pulled the cork and poured into two dusty glasses, handing one to Rufe. "You talkin' about Dan Laskovy?"

Rufe nodded, sniffing the whiskey. He tasted it and made a face as Peevy grinned.

"Terrible, ain't it?" He drank his in one gulp.

Rufe put the glass down and fished for the makin's. "When you goin' to town next?"

"What you want?"

"Figger to write to Dan."

"Well, I c'n go tomorra. Need beans and salt; could use some vinegar and sassafras . . ."

"Good. Get all the papers, too. What you got for supper?"

* * *

In the morning Peevy hooked up the mules to a buck-board and climbed over the wheel, grunting with the effort. He looked at Rufe. "Be gone a day or two likely."

"Don't forget to mail that . . ."

Peevy patted the pocket with the letter. "Jesus, you worse'n a woman." He lifted the reins and bawled at the team. The wagon clattered away from the house.

With Peevy gone, Rufe opened the three windows and the door, hoping to get some of the smell out. He took a burning branch and walked around the room with it. In an hour the room smelled some better, but not much. The stink had probably soaked into the wood and stone and would never come out.

At midday he took a can of beans outside and ate it sitting on the steps. It would take Dan four or five days to get the letter—with luck. And another week and a half to come here to the cabin.

Rufe sighed. He was going to have to smell Peevy for another two or three weeks. The things he put up with . . .

Chapter Six

THEY rode to Lichfield and arrived about noon, getting down in front of a restaurant on the main street. As they entered and took a table Laredo smiled at Deputy Homer Cross who sat across the room glowering at them.

Cross was with two other men and must have said something to them; they both turned and studied Laredo and Pete. They were both lanky and brown, wearing checked shirts and jeans. Neither was armed, and they looked, as Pete said, like drifters.

Laredo ignored them. He ordered boiled pork, corn bread, and coffee. Pete rolled a cigarette while they waited.

Cross and his friends were about finished and got up to go as Laredo and Pete were pitching in. Cross came to their table and looked down at them.

"We got an ordinance against wearin' guns in town."

"We're lawmen," Laredo said pleasantly.

"That don't cut no corn. You want to give up the guns?"

Laredo pushed his chair back. "If you want them, come and take them." He looked at Cross. Pete went on eating.

Cross glared at him for a moment, pressing his thin lips tightly together, then turned and walked out stiffly.

"Unhappy *hombre*," Pete said mildly. "Big frog in a little puddle and don't like other frogs coming in."

"Speak for yourself, *amigo*."

Pete made a noise like a frog, and Laredo laughed.

They went out to the street and stood in the shade while Pete rolled a brown cigarette. A slouch-seated horseman rode past, and several wooden carts drawn by oxen came into town to their right.

Laredo got out one of the photos Fleming had sent them. "Wonder where the Porter boys are hanging out?"

Pete took the photo, looking at it with his head on one side. "Haven't heard a thing about them for a spell. Maybe they went east for a fling. We would have heard if they got dead."

"Yes." He put the photo away. "Any use our asking Deputy Cross again for information?"

"I doubt it. Let's find us a newspaper."

The general store had half a dozen that had been sent from the county seat, Giler, only yesterday. They bought one and read it sitting on a bench in front of the store. On the second page was an item about Thelma Wicker. She had been taken into custody when she refused to give any information concerning her fugitive husband, Rufus Wicker.

"Well, the law sniffed her out," Pete said in surprise. "She's in jail in Giler for the time being. It says here they'll hold her until she talks."

"That could take a while. Where's Giler?"

"It also says the federal government is interested in Wicker. Does that mean us?"

"Probably." Laredo got up and went inside to ask the store owner about Giler. He came back and sat down. "Giler's west of here a day's ride. Will Rufe try to get her out?"

"He might—depending on the jail." Pete put the paper down and yawned. "You want to go to Giler?"

"Might as well. We're not doing a hell of a lot of good here. Right now Thelma is our only contact with Wicker."

Pete unfolded the wanted poster of Wicker and studied it. "This likeness isn't worth a stale tortilla. Why don't we get some posters printed using the photo John Fleming sent us?"

"Very good idea!" Laredo got up again and went into the store. He was back in a moment. "No printer in town. The closest is Longworth or Giler."

"So let's go to Giler."

It was an uneventful trip. They met no one at all and came onto the town as they rounded a hill. The sky was like tarnished silver with gray clouds on the horizon. The first few houses were unpainted shacks; a few dogs barked and yapped at them, then gave up and went back to the shade. The false fronts were dusty and curling from the heat. The bank was on a corner, a red brick building with an iron overhang. The stores were jumbled, one after the other in a quagmire of signs. Men were hammering in a freight yard, and a stagecoach came rattling into town and pulled up as people spilled out to greet whoever stepped down.

Laredo and Pete halted before a print shop and got down stiffly. The print shop was noisy as a press clanked monotonously: a boy was turning a wheel and staring at them.

The owner was named Elmer Gargan. He was a stocky man with silver-rimmed glasses who wiped his hands on a rag as they showed him the photo of Wicker and the wanted poster.

Laredo said, "We want this photo on the poster instead. Can you do it?"

"Certainly. Who pays for it? If it's the government, I don't want the job."

"Why not?"

"Because they too slow with payment."

"Then we'll pay," Laredo said, "and bill the government."

"How many copies?"

Laredo looked at Pete. "Five hundred?"

Gargan said, "Hardly worth the trouble, five hundred."

"A thousand, then. When can we have them?"

Gargan glanced at the printing press. "Couple days." He led the way to the front of the room and sat at a desk. "Give me five dollars on account . . ."

Outside on the boardwalk Pete said, "What're we going to do with a thousand copies?"

Peevy returned with the wagon late in the afternoon of the second day. Rufe helped him carry in boxes of supplies, then sat outside with the several newspapers.

He was disgusted to read that Thelma was in the Giler jail charged with withholding information. They had no goddam business holding her! He ought to go and bust her out!

Peevy thought it was a dumb idea. "That's exactly what they want you t'do. Why the hell you figger they pulled her in? Just so they could get to you."

Rufe frowned, but it did make sense.

"Besides, they got to turn her loose," Peevy argued. "What's she done? Was she with you in the bank?"

"Hell, no."

"Then they can't hold her."

Rufe shook the paper. "It says they holding her for information."

"How the hell they know what she knows? Maybe she don't know anything! You tell her anything?"

"Not much."

"So they going to look inside her head? They have to turn her loose. She got the money for a lawyer?"

"Of course."

Peevy spread his hands "Then she probably out by now. She's home cookin' greens and corn pone. No use you worrying. Ain't a damn thing you c'n do about it 'cept grind your teeth."

Rufe sighed deeply. Damn the law. . . .

Peevy went to town again in a week, but there was no letter in the basket for him.

The letter from Laskovy didn't arrive until the second week. Then all it said was that he was on his way. He didn't show up in person for another nine days.

"What you got in mind?"

Rufe said, "Come in and set for crissakes. You got to get back to that girl in Pueblo?"

Dan put his horse in the corral. "You got something cased?"

"No, I haven't. We got to talk."

"What about?"

Rufe drew his fingers through the curling edges of his dark hair. "You'n me, we rammin' around casual-like, doin' this and that. But I been figgering: we ain't getting any younger." He put out his arm and drew Laskovy aside. They walked away from the house. "I told Peevy we made a poor hit at Ruskin. Ain't none of his business anyways."

"That's right."

Rufe felt for the makin's. "Like I said, we ain't gettin' any younger. I figger it's time for us to make one'r two good strikes and quit."

Laskovy nodded. He watched Rufe roll a brown cigarette, lick the flap, and strike a match. He would sure as hell like that. Settle down without a six-gun under your pillow. Beatrice, the girl in Pueblo, would like that, too. He said, "But we'd have to get clean out of this country. Go somewhere—"

"Jeezus! It's a big world. With money from a good strike'r two we could go anywheres we want. Way the hell the other side of Kansas City."

Dan took a long breath. "All right, where we going to find us a big strike?"

"Well, we'd have to go looking."

"You figgering to take a bank?"

"Maybe." Rufe puffed and stepped on the remains of the cigarette. "They's money in banks."

"We'd need more'n just us two, then . . . for a big bank."

"What about a train?" Rufe grinned. "With the right information we could get rich. Them trains carries a hell of a lot of cash sometimes."

"You thinking of the Porter boys?"

Rufe nodded. "They knows how to do 'er."

"It's a wider split."

"It could be worth it. And the more of us, the safer."

Dan gazed at the other. "You talked to the Porter bunch?"

"No."

"Can you get ahold of them?"

"I think so." Rufe indicated the house. "Let's go back and eat. We can think about it and talk later. All right?"

Dan nodded.

"And don't say nothing in front of Peevy."

"You don't trust 'im?"

"It don't pay to trust nobody—except me and you."

Chapter Seven

Laredo paid two small boys to distribute some of the posters in Giler. He put the rest of them in a cloth sack. They would distribute them in every town they came to. It might help to stir up something. A thousand dollars for each of the outlaws was a hell of a lot of money. It was to be doubted that five people in the county had that much cash on hand.

The jailhouse in Giler was mostly stone with a log roof. When they went inside, a deputy informed them the sheriff was away. He looked at their credentials, said yes, Mrs. Rufe Wicker was still in the jail, but they would probably be letting her go in a few days.

"Her lawyer's been raisin' a fuss."

Laredo asked, "Has she told you anything at all about Rufe?"

The deputy, a slim, middle-aged man, shook his head. "Swears at us a lot. . . . Smokes cigars, too. Be glad when we get shut of her. Sheriff give orders no one was to talk to her. . . ."

They thanked the man and went out to the street. Pete suggested they follow her when she was released. "She may go to meet Rufe."

The county seat was a small town, dominated by the courthouse and other county buildings, including the jail. There were two hotels, three dance halls, all saloon-connected, and seven saloons altogether. There was also a theater, advertising a new play: *A Lover's Lament*.

At the Yearling Hotel the desk clerk, a talkative young man, informed them it was a slow time. "No hangings scheduled this month. Folks comes in from all around, have themselves a picnic when we got three or four."

"That's a shame," Pete said. "No entertainment."

The clerk glanced at him. "You-all want to sign your names, gents?" He turned the register around to face them. "One dollar a day." He laid two keys on the counter.

Laredo bought a copy of the Giler *Observer* and read it in the room. There was nothing about Rufus or the robbery-murders in Ruskin.

But there was a paragraph, picked up from a Kansas City newspaper, reporting that Gus Porter, of the notorious Porter gang, had been taken into custody in St. Joseph, then released for lack of evidence.

He showed the item to Pete. "Maybe Rufe went to St. Joseph. He could be going into the train-robbing business. What d'you think?"

"A good supposition. But they won't stay in St. Joseph. This paper is three days old, and the item from Kansas City is probably ten days old. They could be anywhere by now."

That of course was true, Laredo reflected. He could even be here in Giler. *With* the Porter gang.

Except that the nearest rails were at Hartwell, which was on a spur line. The kind of train the Porters would be looking for was one that carried important goods, such as the Fort Haynes and Western.

He mentioned it to Pete, who nodded. "But we're five steps behind them—assuming they're about to hold up a train. They could be watching a variety show in Chicago."

"You have an annoying habit of being right."

Pete grinned. "I am a college graduate."

"Let's go to supper. You can show me which fork to use."

The deputy at the jail agreed to let them know when Mrs. Thelma Wicker was about to be turned loose. She had

had her buckboard and team delivered to the jail and would return home in it. She had also hired a young man to drive her there.

So when she left the jail precincts they were waiting. The road to Saylor was reasonably well marked, and they were able to keep the wagon in view by means of a pair of binoculars and were not noticed.

It was a four-day journey, and Thelma Wicker did not meet her husband. It was very discouraging.

They bedded down in the trees and watched the house. "Give Rufe a chance," Laredo said. "Maybe he's on his way here."

But in the morning Thelma hooked up the buckboard again and drove into Saylor. She had paid off the young driver the day before. She bought a box full of supplies at the general store, then picked up a letter at the post office.

Laredo and Pete watched her slit it open and read it as she sat on the buckboard seat, their hands itching to get hold of it. She read the letter twice, smiled, put it away, and drove home.

The postmaster could not—or would not—tell them who the letter had been from.

Rufus wrote a letter to Gus Porter, in care of Henry Whitaker at the Alamo Saloon in Fort Griffin. He put one envelope inside another with a note to Henry to forward the letter if he knew where Gus was. Henry could be depended upon.

Peevy had to make another trip to town to post it. Rufe knew it might cause talk, Peevy showing up twice in a week, but there was no help for it. He made up a story for Peevy to tell, but Peevy would probably forget. . . . The old man was getting more grumbling and forgetful with every day that passed.

It might easily take a month for Gus Porter to get the letter, let alone answer it, and he was beginning to feel itchy again. He and Dan decided to ride south where there were a number of towns; maybe one would have a fat bank just waiting for them to come and pluck it.

According to the map, Doren was a good-size burg. It was four or five sleeps away, and neither of them had been there.

They packed food in sacks and set out early one morning, telling Peevy they were pointing west. Well out of sight of the house they turned south. By nightfall they were out of the hills, and camped on the edge of the prairie in a grove of cottonwoods.

The first habitation they came to was a tiny settlement, a trading post built alongside a creek with a straggle of tents and shacks accompanying it. The entire place looked poor as a spavined mule.

A bartender told them Doren was just down the road, maybe a day and half south. "They's a stage road runs west from Doren. You can't miss it."

The beer tasted bitter, and the deadfall smelled as if a cat had died under the bar. They went out into the air, and Rufe rolled a smoke, passing the papers to Dan. As they rode out they passed some wickiups of braided willow twigs and half a dozen Indian children playing along the creek.

"Damn lonesome country," Rufe said, squinting into the distance. "You ever been east, Dan?"

"Sure. I been to Sedalia."

"Wonder what it's like across the ocean. . . ."

Dan shook his head. "That's too far t'think about. Place is full of them damn foreigners anyhow."

"Like to see some of them French women—what they say, they're something frilly."

"Wimmin is wimmin," Dan said definitively. "They is like cats. All cats is the same in the dark."

Rufe nodded, but he didn't agree. All women were not the same in the dark. At least not in his experience.

The prairie was barren-flat and in places had a baked and curling crust that their horses' feet crackled, cutting through. They crossed a half-mile-wide wash with driftwood strewn along its sides, brought by a spring rise.

When they hit the stage road, it was near dark, and they

were hungry. They camped till morning, then headed east, coming onto a cabin, a line of stock shelters, and a new barn. Nearby was a peeled log house with a shake roof and a barrel for a chimney. A few cows stared at them from beyond a worm fence.

The town was larger than they'd expected; it was the county seat with a three-storied wood-and-brick court-house, tall rounded-top windows, and a fancy copper-domed cupola.

On the street were men in store suits and a clutter of wagon and buggy traffic. There were three banks; the largest was a red-brick building with an iron overhang painted black and a shiny brass kickplate on the wide door. On the two windows were gold-leaf signs: Doren Bank & Trust.

The two other banks were smaller. The town marshal's office was next door to one; the third was between a hardware store and a saloon, The Palace.

They got down and went into the saloon. It smelled of beer and cigar smoke. There was a long bar to the left, with brass spittoons and a polished rail; the backbar had mirrors and small flags, several scalps stretched on willow hoops near a pair of huge longhorns.

A few men were drinking at the bar, a few playing cards, and half a dozen gathered about the gaming tables where the click of ivory balls could be heard. Rufe and Dan ordered beer and stared at the several girls who moved about easily. . . . One of them was dark and slim with swamp-cat eyes. Rufe asked the bartender her name.

"She's Klara," the man said, and smacked his lips.

Dan poked his ribs. "We come here for something else."

"I only asked a question."

"Let's go look at the bank."

They finished the beer. Rufe took one last glance at Klara, and they walked down the block to the Doren Bank & Trust. Inside was a large room with tables and a line of barred windows. Two uniformed guards gazed at everyone who entered.

They drifted out and back to The Palace. "Too damned

many guards," Dan said. "Me, I don't like even odds."

The bank next to The Palace was called the Cattleman's Trust. It had only one guard, a man seated above the tellers' cages with a shotgun across his thighs.

Dan said, "You figger they expecting us?"

Chapter Eight

Laredo and Pete Torres waited in Saylor several days, satisfying themselves Rufe was not in town. They were equally sure he was not at the ranch. So probably the letter his wife had received was from Rufe. They even considered breaking into the house to get it, but certainly Thelma would burn it immediately. After all, she was an outlaw's wife.

They wired John Fleming that they'd lost the trail. Rufe and Dan Laskovy could be anywhere, planning anything. All they could do was wait . . . and hope to get on the trail after the next job.

Fleming agreed. He also had information that Dan Laskovy had been seen in Pueblo but had suddenly disappeared from those environs. Fleming supposed he had gone to join Rufe. And if that were true, the two probably had a job planned. All banks in the area, Fleming said, had been warned about the two bank robbers, and been alerted to take special precautions.

They rode back to Giler and put up at a hotel. Giler was on the telegraph and would get news quickly.

Over supper Pete suggested they not just wait for developments but go out and distribute the new posters in every town they could find. A clear picture of Rufus might easily do more good than pages of words.

Laredo thought it an excellent idea, and they put it into

operation at once. They flipped a coin in the morning and decided to go south.

At the first settlement, a trading post on the prairie, they paid a lad to distribute the posters to every citizen. When he saw the photo, the bartender in the only deadfall swore he had seen the man on the poster only days before.

"He and another *hombre* come in here not more'n a week ago. They was pointin' south. Asked about Doren."

Outside, as they got on the horses, Pete snapped his fingers. "Lady Luck! She's taking sides! Is there a bank in Doren?"

"We'll soon find out."

There were three banks, each one well-guarded. They called on the town marshal, a wiry oldster with gray hair and a six-gun about his slim middle. He looked very competent. But he frowned at the poster. "Haven't seen 'im, but I know the name. I got another poster or two on him."

He tacked the poster to the wall, nodding as Pete explained they would have them distributed in the town. Several boys passed them out to every house and store in the town. Wicker had a distinctive appearance, with his beak nose and long hair. Someone ought to remember him . . . if he had been in Doren.

And someone did.

His name, as he told the marshal, was Tim Harris. He was a shabbily dressed older man with steel-rimmed specs and squinty eyes. He pointed to the poster on the wall. "That true, about the reward?"

"Course it's true. You know something?"

"What I have to do to collect the reward?"

The marshal let out his breath. "You got to tell me, that's all."

"If I tell you, then you'll go get him and collect it."

"For crissake! I'll go get him, but you'll collect it." The marshal led Harris to the poster. "Lookit that. It says for information, don't it? Ain't that what it says?"

Harris nodded.

"So tell me. You seen Wicker?"

"He been living at my boardinghouse."

"Is he alone?"

Harris shook his head. "There's another gent with him."

"What's he look like?"

Harris described Laskovy, down to his tight little ears.

"All right. Were they in the house when you left?"

"I dunno. They mighta been in their room."

Harris demanded a note saying he had told the marshal where to find Wicker, and watched the marshal sign it with a sigh. He put the note away carefully, smiled, and went out.

The marshal sent a boy for Laredo and Pete Torres.

When they came into his office, he told them about Harris. "Wicker and Laskovy are at Mrs. Broome's boardinghouse on Allen Street . . . at least Harris thinks they're still there."

Laredo asked, "Have you got a deputy?"

"Yes, but he ain't in town."

"Can you deputize three or four men?"

The marshal nodded. "What you figgering?"

"Surround the boardinghouse and ask them to come out nice and peaceable."

The older man nodded again. "When you want to do this?"

"As soon as possible," Laredo said. "When can you get the men together?"

"Give me a few hours." The marshal pulled out a turnip watch and studied it. "We'll meet later tonight . . . right here in the office."

"Good."

The girl in The Palace saloon, Klara, was a piece of fluff. Rufe had gone back and taken her upstairs and spent three hours wallowing in her charms. The next day he had spent another two.

They ought to be moving on, Dan said. But of course he didn't know what Klara was like. And he resented her.

Rufe knew the other was right: they would take no bank in this town . . . but he hated to leave her, just yet. It was

47

lonely as hell out on the prairie. His memories of her or of Thelma could not hold a candle to reality.

Then Dan told him there was an old geezer at the boardinghouse giving him funny looks.

"What you mean, funny looks?"

"Like maybe he recognizes you or me. . . . There's posters out, you know."

It bothered Rufe. If the law got their hands on him, there was no telling what they'd do. He said to Dan, "Then we'll move out in the morning—early. Get us some vittles in a sack, and we'll clear out before sunup."

"That's better. . . ."

Rufe went to see Klara for the last time. He didn't tell her so, and he stayed extra-long.

When he walked back to the boardinghouse very late, he felt uneasy. Something was wrong. Stopping, he peered around and listened several times on the way . . . and could see or hear nothing untoward. But his outlaw's feelers or instincts were at a high pitch.

He was to meet Dan in the alley behind Mrs. Broome's. Dan would have the horses and their possibles. He slid into the alley and halted, listening. It was dark as the inside of a cat. Dan would be about a block down. Rufe wished suddenly they had agreed to meet in a better place. He tried to walk silently, then halted, hearing horses.

It sounded like two horses moving at a walk—probably Dan getting impatient and coming to meet him. Rufe took a step, then the dark was rent with an orange blossom, and a bullet screamed past him. Someone yelled.

Rufe heard Dan's voice calling out, and he answered and ran forward. Dan materialized out of the gloom on his mount, leading Rufe's bay. Another shot blasted the silences, and the bullet rapped into a tree somewhere to their right. Rufe clambered aboard the bay. "Let's get outa here!"

He followed Dan, galloping into the dark as two more shots cracked around them.

Dan turned into a dark street, and they ran at a headlong pace, bypassing the main business street, heading into the open. Behind them several men shouted, but no one followed on horseback. Were they a posse?

The street they were on petered out, and they were suddenly on the prairie sod with the glimmering lantern lights of the town behind them.

They reined in, catching their breaths. "You hit?" Dan asked.

"Never touched me." Rufe got down and felt the bay's chest and hindquarters. "Hard to shoot straight in the goddam dark. Who were they?"

"Probably a bunch tryin' to collect the reward. I heard somebody walking in the dry weeds, so I come down the alley. I figger they were going to move in at first light."

"Probably was," Rufe agreed. Luck was still with them. Another fifteen minutes, and they'd have had Dan surrounded.

Dan studied the dark sky. "We best move our butts. It'll be light in an hour or so. Which way you want to point?"

"Why not go west?"

"Suits me. Them fellers shootin' at us was mighty nervous . . . easy spooked."

Rufe nudged the bay horse. "If they come after us, we'll show 'em what shootin' is."

The marshal rounded up four young men for the posse. One was a stable helper, two were employed as wagon drivers, and the fourth did odd jobs. It took the marshal more than three hours to get them together and they were picked mostly because each had a gun, a pistol, or a rifle, or could borrow one.

It was very late in the afternoon by then, and all four were more interested in supper than in listening to instructions.

Laredo despaired, looking at them. He and Pete could probably do the job better alone. But when he mentioned it to the marshal, the older man shook his head. This was his town, and he would do it his way. After all, he was the one who had to answer to the town council.

The marshal decided they would go in shortly before first light.

Laredo explained to them how they would do it, drawing a diagram on the marshal's desk. Three would go in the front and four in the back. They would get everyone out of the house as quietly as possible. . . .

But when the time came, nothing happened as planned.

The possemen had approached the house like a herd of hungry elephants—despite Pete Torres's objections, and had flushed out a man on a horse, leading another horse. Pete had not seen the horseman and was disgusted when the possemen began firing in the night.

He told Laredo later it was as if they had been in cahoots with Rufe and Dan. Laredo thought they were only making sure their quarry was well warned so they, the inexperienced possemen, would not be shot at.

But the upshot was Rufus and Dan Laskovy got clean away. They questioned Mrs. Broome and one or two others in the boardinghouse, and there was no doubt the two had been Wicker and Laskovy. Tim Harris was disgusted, and he had every right: he had been done out of several thousand dollars.

It was guesswork as to where the two fugitives had gone. It was clear where they had left the town, but then they could easily have taken any direction. Perhaps a skilled tracker could have made something of the myriad tracks and signs on the ground . . . but maybe not.

Laredo and Pete returned to Doren and wired John Fleming. They had bad news again. But they had been close. . . .

Chapter Nine

RUFUS and Dan Laskovy headed west and in a day came across a line of telegraph poles. The poles marched away to the northwest bearing the talking wire and, after a brief discussion, the two men followed them.

The wire led them to Haskins, a shacky town that owed its existence to a spring-fed lake and an ancient north-south trail. It had grown to house some two thousand souls including perhaps two dozen women—not counting dance hall girls and those living in the line houses.

They got down in front of the telegraph office and sent a wire to Henry Whitaker at the Alamo Saloon in Fort Griffin.

They had a reply in three hours. Whitaker informed them GP was in Lyden and would wait for them there.

"Gus Porter's in Lyden," Dan said, reading the yellow sheet. "How far's that?"

"Three, four days." Rufe leaned on the hitchrack and looked at the town. "What say we sleep in a bed tonight and hit out in the morning. My horse is favorin' his right leg some. Might be throwing a shoe. You go on to the hotel. I'll find me a blacksmith."

There was one on the only side street. His name was Bilkins—printed in big block letters by some unsteady hand on the side of the building. Bilkins was a big man, completely bald, his head shining with sweat. He wiped his hands on his leather apron and looked at the bay horse.

"Take 'im across there and walk 'im back. . . ."

Rufe led the animal across the street and back.

Bilkins nodded. He patted the bay's chest, rubbing his hand down the dusty shoulder and down to the cannon bone. He lifted the hoof and looked at it closely.

"Toe's worn. He got swing-off trouble." He removed the old shoe and took a stiff brush to the hoof, then pared the toe to receive the new shoe.

"They a newspaper in town?" Rufe asked, watching the smith heat a new shoe.

"Nope. We gets one from Buckhorn ever' week. Only three, four days old. If they got any left, they'll be over at the gen'ral store." The blacksmith put the hoof down. "All right, take him over there and walk him back again."

Rufe led the horse back as the blacksmith squatted to watch, then nodded. "He be fine now."

Rufe paid the man and rode to the general store. They still had three copies of the Buckhorn *Democrat*. He took one to the hotel, put the bay in the stable, and read the paper from front to back. His name was not mentioned. There was nothing about the little fracas at Doren. He felt a vague disappointment at being overlooked.

Dan read the paper in the restaurant and folded it up with a grunt. His attitude conveyed he was happy their pictures were not being plastered everywhere.

They ate their steaks and went back to the hotel . . . and did not notice the man who stared at them and followed them, making sure they went to the hotel.

Then he hurried to the deputy's office. "I just seen Rufus Wicker!"

The deputy was a short, red-faced man named Hector Willis. "You damn sure?"

"Course I'm damn sure. A thousand dollars sure! The *Democrat* printed his picture last week."

"Where'd you see him?"

"He was in the rest'rant with another *hombre*. They went to the hotel."

"The other one, what'd he look like?"

" 'Bout my size—"

The deputy fussed in his desk and brought out a sheaf of wanted sheets. Riffling through them, he pulled out one and showed it to the other. "That him?"

"Yes. That's him."

"Goddam! Wicker and Laskovy! They both in the hotel now?"

"Yes."

"Sonofabitch!" Hector Willis had never been involved in a serious crime before. The sheriff had stationed him in Haskins because it was a quiet town where nothing much ever happened. Willis was not the brightest young man the sheriff had ever seen, but how much damage could he do in a place like Haskins?

"What you goin' to do?"

Deputy Willis shook his head. He had to figure something; but those two in the hotel were damn dangerous killers. The wanted sheets were specific on that point. He had been a deputy only a year and a half. Did he have the authority to raise a posse? He had never asked the sheriff. Of course the question had never come up before.

But was he going into the hotel alone? He could not see himself doing that. He would have to raise a posse!

"Well, what are you going to do?" the informant asked again. "The reward is—"

"Damn the reward! Why'n't you go on home," Willis snapped. "This's police business from now on."

"Don't you forget who told you them two is—"

"I won't forget." Willis motioned the other out. Then he sat down to think. The hotel was a terrible bad place to try to arrest the two outlaws. If any shooting started, a lot of innocent folks could be hurt.

Their horses were probably in the hotel stable. What if he had it surrounded and when the two came out—Willis snapped his fingers. That was a good plan!

But when would they come out? They might stay in the town for a week. What would the sheriff do in his place?

He rose and went to the door, thinking to wire the sheriff; then a picture of the old man came into his head. The

53

sheriff was one of the hard-bitten old-timers, afraid of nothing, contemptuous of anyone not as hard as nails. No, if he wanted to remain a deputy, he had best do this himself. If he asked advice, the sheriff would know him to be weak.

It took an hour to get five men together, all armed, all with a few drinks in them, but all willing. Willis did not tell them Rufe Wicker was in town. He told them he was merely going after a lawbreaker who happened to be in the hotel. None of the five wondered aloud why it would take six men to arrest one.

Hector Willis left them outside on the walk while he entered the hotel to talk to the desk clerk. It was late, and there was no one in the small lobby.

"Let me see your register." Willis turned it around and read the names. There was no Wicker and no Laskovy. Well, of course they had used false names. He described the two to the desk clerk.

The clerk, named Harry Barnes, was seventy-three, with thick glasses. He shook his head as Willis described the men. "I don't remember nobody like that."

Willis stared at the glasses, realizing the clerk probably could not see across the desk. He had a sinking feeling in his gut. He certainly could not turn out everyone in the hotel—it would be dangerous as hell to do so.

What could he do but wait? He went back out to the five men and explained the circumstance. They would have to surround the stable and wait.

They followed him around to the dark stable, muttering among themselves. Willis placed the men where he thought they would be most effective. He put himself near the rear door of the hotel and settled down to wait.

When he made the rounds of his five possemen an hour later, he discovered they had all slipped away. He was alone.

Dan Laskovy woke at four in the morning . . . by his old silver watch. He slid out of bed and woke Rufe. "Time to go . . ."

They dressed and went downstairs and out the back way to the stable. Rufe lit a lantern and hung it by its wire, and they saddled the horses and tied on the blanket rolls and food sacks.

As they opened the alley door someone fired at them. Five rifle shots splintered the door in a wide pattern.

Rufe swore, hauling out his Colt pistol. The sniper was standing in the middle of the alley, fifty feet or so down, a cloud of gray smoke rising about him. He fired again as Rufe snapped two shots at him, then dug spurs into the bay horse. Dan fired at the man as he galloped from the stable following Rufe.

Deputy Willis emptied the rifle at the rapidly disappearing two, swearing as it clicked empty. Neither man had dropped. He had probably missed with every shot.

But they had missed him, too. Of course they had been surprised and on horseback, shooting into the dark.

Well, at least he could tell the old sheriff he had faced two killers alone and unaided. He hadn't stopped them, but how many others in his place would have?

It made him feel some better.

Rufus and Dan galloped out of town following the road northeast. Who the hell had pulled down on them? It couldn't be the town law, Dan thought; he'd have had a posse. It must have been some citizen trying for the rewards.

They stopped and examined the horses. No harm done. The gent, whoever he was, had been a terrible shot . . . or he had been so spooked he couldn't hit the ground with a bottle of rotgut.

But no one followed them. The law didn't have a posse ready. "We got to stay outa these goddam towns for a while," Rufe said. "Folks got nothing better to do than sit around and look at pictures of us."

Dan nodded. "Maybe if we get into another line of work, like the train business . . ."

* * *

Lyden was a good-sized town, as large as Doren, perhaps not as bustling, but on the Fort Brill and Southern Railway. The Porter brothers were staying in the Travelers' Home Inn, a sprawling structure of brown-stained wood a block from the railroad station. It had a long-settled look with wide verandas and shrubbery. The whitewashed stable behind the hotel was half as long and well-tended.

The Porters were expecting them. Gus Porter was a burly man with dark hair and heavy brows. He had the air of a man who was in firm command; his black eyes were steady, and his big fists looked capable of backing up his words.

He and his brother, Quinn, had a suite. Quinn was younger and slightly thinner, but anyone seeing them together would know they were brothers. They were known at the hotel as cattlemen and were registered under the name Packer.

Another of the gang was with them, a younger man named Phil Bowers. He had a room down the hall and was just out of prison; he still had the prison pallor and nervous habits. Harvey Elland and George Docker, longtime members of the Porter gang, were still in the East. Gus said he did not expect them to come west for some time.

Quinn set out drinks and cigars on a silver tray, offering to send downstairs for food if they were hungry. He and Quinn had been in St. Louis, Gus told them, seeing the sights and spending the money that burned their pockets. They had done a very successful job six months past, but now it was time to get down to serious business again. The money was almost gone.

"It's the Fort Brill and Southern we got in mind," Gus said. "That's why we're here in Lyden. We've got a clerk on the payroll who works for the army at Fort Logan. He sends us information."

"What kind of information?"

"About what's on the trains."

Quinn said, "This time it's a big one. We're going after a big haul." He pointed his glass at them. "You want in?"

"We need two men," Gus said. "Five of us all together should handle it nicely."

Rufe grinned. "That's why we're here. We want a big one, too." He glanced at Dan, who nodded.

"Then you're in," Gus said, grinning back. He leaned forward, and they clinked glasses. "Glad to have you aboard."

Dan asked, "What's the job?"

Quinn said quickly, "We're going after a payroll."

Rufe was astonished. "A payroll!?" There wasn't a business within five hundred miles, including the railroad, that had enough employees to make a payroll robbery worthwhile to five men.

The expression on his face made Gus chuckle. "We're talking about an *army* payroll. A couple of thousand men! The army pays off every month. Thousands and thousands of dollars—in cash!" He rubbed his hands together.

Rufe smiled. "In cash?"

Chapter Ten

LAREDO and Pete Torres rode out onto the prairie a mile
or two and halted. The sod was wet with dew as if it had
rained. The lopsided moon was ice-white, and the ap-
proaching sun sent long fingers to flush the sky.

They walked the horses through several maverick
clumps of cottonwood scrub and turned back toward the
town. There was no telling where Rufe and Dan had gone.
They might even have split up to confuse pursuers.

They might be smart to stay in Doren a spell, where
they'd be near the telegraph. If they went chasing off
somewhere, it would probably be the wrong direction. . . .

Pete said sensibly, "Let's have breakfast. A man thinks
better with a full stomach."

They put the horses in the livery and walked across the
street to a restaurant. It was frustrating to do nothing.
Could they go back and question Thelma Wicker again?
She might let drop something . . . and she might not.

It seemed likely that since Rufe and Dan Laskovy were
together, they were planning another bank holdup.

But where? There were a hundred banks within a week's
ride; of course few of them were large enough to attract a
man like Rufe. The bank at Ruskin must have been on the
borderline.

Over coffee Pete mentioned the Porter gang. "Are they
out of jail? Is it possible Rufe could join with them?"

They decided to wire John Fleming.

Fleming's answer was interesting. Gus Porter and his brother, Quinn, had been seen in Chicago recently. It was not known whether or not they were still there. Another of the gang, Phil Bowers, had served his term and had been released from Leavenworth Prison two weeks past. He had gone west immediately and had been tailed to Lyden, where he had eluded the tail.

"Lyden," Pete said. "Where's that?"

They looked it up on a map. It was a town about the size of Doren, on a railroad.

"Probably a couple of banks there," Laredo said. "It's cattle country to the south. They'll drive to the railroad, and the banks will have fortunes in the safes. . . ."

"This is summer," Pete said. "They won't drive cattle again till fall. This Bowers—maybe he grew up near there. He got out of prison and went home."

"Fleming would have said so."

"Ummm."

"So what do you think? He's meeting the Porter brothers?"

Laredo shrugged. "He could be. But that's not the question . . . are Rufe and Dan meeting them?"

"There are a lot of ifs in this business," Pete observed. "Should we go to Lyden or back to Saylor? We *know* Thelma is in Saylor."

"And we know she won't talk to us."

Pete sighed deeply.

Laredo said, "I think we ought to go to Lyden."

"By way of Saylor?"

"What if we flip a coin?"

Pete dug a cartridge from his belt and held out his fist. "Lead up we go Saylor. Primer up we go to Lyden. You call it."

"Primer up."

Pete opened his fist to show the primer up.

Gus Porter said, "We haven't worked it all out yet, not all the details. The army paymaster sends the money in the express car every month. It comes from the headquarters in Eagleton to the army center at Fort Logan, which is a big place. It's five, six miles out of Daleyville."

"We been arguing about taking the shipment between Daleyville and the fort," Quinn said. "Gus wants to take it off the train."

"More leeway if we do."

"Maybe. But it'll be harder."

Gus waved his big hand. He had a map, which he spread on a table, holding the corners down with glasses and a bottle. "Here's Eagleton. . . ." His finger traced the black lines. "And this's the railroad. The shipment is put off the train here, at Daleyville." He tapped the map with the finger. "But it's met by a bunch of cavalry."

"Twelve men," Quinn said.

"All right. But there's only six Pinkertons in the express car. And we got two hunnerd miles between them two towns . . . as agin only five or six."

Gus scratched a match and lit a cigar as Quinn said, "But there's a stretch of badlands right here beside the trail to the fort. We raid the wagon train and we get away into the badlands. It'll take the cavalry hours and hours to find out we got the treasure, and by then we'll be long gone."

"What happens to the twelve soldiers?" Dan asked.

Quinn smiled, pointed his finger, and said, "Bang bang bang."

"Ambush," Phil Bowers said, speaking for the first time. "They won't expect us."

"The plan'll work that way," Gus conceded, waving the cigar, "but I think it's less risk t'other way. What you figger, Rufe?"

Rufe frowned at the map. After a moment he touched it at Daleyville. "Worries me some about all them soldiers bein' so close. You said a couple thousand of 'em?"

"They're mostly infantry," Quinn said quickly. "There's only one or two troops of cavalry, and a girl rollin' a hoop could go faster'n them."

"Where'll you go after you leave the badlands?"

"Here," Quinn said. His finger traced a line. "We ride

east to this here town, Lee's Ferry. We bury the money in the cemetery just outside of town, then we scatter."

"Bury it!" Dan said, astonished.

"No goddam evidence," Quinn explained. "We scatter, and we come back in two months, dig it up, and divvy."

Rufe accepted a cigar from Gus. He wasn't wild about that aspect: bury it and come back later. He lit the cigar and puffed hard. But the no-evidence thing was a good touch. If they happened to get rounded up, they could always say "Who, me?"

A jury was sure to let them go if they had no loot.

Gus didn't care for the burying idea either. "If I'm gonna steal it, I want it with me." He stood over the map. "We have a wagon and team waiting along the tracks. We cut the express car loose and no worries about soldiers."

Rufe looked at him. "Cut the car loose?"

Gus nodded and pointed. "Phil knows how t'do that. He spent a year'r two working on the railroad."

Phil said, "They'll have the express car just ahead of the caboose."

Rufe said, "What about the six Pinkertons?"

"They'll be in the express car or in one of the other cars. Usually they's always four in the express car." Gus smiled around the cigar. "There's five of us to take care o'them. And we'll have surprise on our side." He paused for effect. "And dynamite."

Rufus stared at him.

"Dynamite," Gus said again. "We'll blow the goddam door off the express car."

Dan asked, "Who knows about dynamite?"

Gus shrugged. "What's to know? You light the fuse. It goes bang."

Rufe made a face. "It sounds pretty good." He glanced at Quinn. "What's wrong with it?"

"Nothing. We've done it before."

Gus said, "He likes to try something different alla time. He's had two wives—"

"All right!" Quinn cut in. "We'll do it your way." He went across the room and poured a drink.

61

"It's three weeks before the next shipment," Gus told them. "I suggest we scatter and meet here in two weeks. That all right?" He looked round at them. "From now on, if we meet on the street, we don't know one another."

Rufe nodded. Jesus! Three weeks! He glanced at Dan. What would they do for three weeks? He wished he were back in Doren with Klara. But it wouldn't pay to make the long ride to Doren and back.

When he and Dan got outside, Dan said, "This's a good big town. Whyn't we just stay here? We can change our appearance a little bit. . . ."

"Yeah, I didn't figger on no three weeks' wait."

"Think I'll grow me a beard. I had one before once. They scratch like hell, though. You want to go to a hotel or a boardinghouse?"

"Boardinghouse's cheaper."

"But you're throwed together closer with people."

Rufe sighed. "We could camp out in the sticks, too. Hell, I think I wanna stay in the goddam hotel even if it is a dollar a day. What you say?"

"All right. You want to go to the same hotel?"

Rufe nodded. "Like Gus says, we won't know each other. You grow the beard, and I'll get m'hair cut."

They put up at a small hotel, the Anderson, run by Obe Anderson, a big, blond Swede who had been born in New York. They went in at different times and had rooms on different floors. The hotel had three, with a stable out back.

Rufe's room was square, with two tapestried-seat chairs, a large mirror fixed to the wall, and a squeaky bed. When he complained, Anderson said they all squeaked.

But he liked the hotel because the Red Horse Saloon was next door, and one of the girls reminded him of Klara. Her name was Adele. He told her he was an iron-goods manufacturer in town waiting for his partner to show up. They were thinking of establishing a new factory in the West. Somehow she got the idea he was wealthy.

It made his stay very pleasant.

Chapter Eleven

IT was a long, weary way to Lyden. For the last fifty miles or so they followed the steel rails, as others had done. There was a well-worn trail beside the tracks.

But at last they came to the shacks and tar-paper sheds, then a few houses, and finally the town buildings loomed up in the dusk. It was a larger burg than they'd expected, a division point on the railroad with yards and roundhouses on the outskirts.

They got down tired and crotch-sore and had supper in a restaurant, put their horses in the nearest livery, and bedded down in an empty stall.

In the morning Laredo rounded up several young boys and had them deliver wanted posters up and down the main street and to all the houses in town. It took several days and used up all the posters they had.

However, there were two printers in town, and they had another thousand made.

The third day brought results. A man brought one of the posters to the town marshal's office. "I seen this feller. How d'I collect the reward?"

"You collect it when we bring him in and convict him. Where is he?"

"I seen him at a saloon . . . fifteen minutes ago."

The marshall sent for Laredo and Pete Torres, and they

met at the saloon with the informant. The man looked over the bat-wing doors.

"He's at the end of the bar. Gent with the flat hat on."

Laredo entered, followed by Pete and the marshal. As he got close Laredo halted and glanced at Pete. It was not Wicker. The man had a resemblance, but it was not Wicker. He was pale and had small, almost dainty hands and was dressed in a store suit.

In the street outside, Laredo shook his head at the informant. "You picked the wrong man. Sorry."

The marshal watched the dejected citizen shamble away. "We'll prob'ly get more of them. . . ."

"I doubt if Wicker will hang out in a bar," Pete said. "But he's got to live somewhere."

"You-all sure he's in this town?"

"No, we're not," Laredo replied. "I wish to hell we were."

He and Pete went to look at the banks in town; there were two. The security precautions were good—armed, uniformed guards and shotgun guards near the tellers' cages. Maybe half a dozen determined men might shoot their way in, but that hadn't been Wicker's way in the past. He had preferred smaller, quiet banks with little or no security.

When they'd asked him, the marshal hadn't known Phil Bowers; there was no Bowers family in town to his knowledge. The police tail had lost Bowers in Lyden, but that did not mean Bowers was still in town. He might well have gone on. He might be meeting the Porter brothers somewhere else—and Rufe and Dan Laskovy, too.

Outside of passing out the posters there was little they could do. John Fleming had told them there were no photographs of the Porter brothers available. They had both been in jail, but all jails did not photograph prisoners. And their descriptions could easily fit a thousand men.

The posters with the photograph of Rufe Wicker were everywhere in town. Dan, with a scraggly beard and store clothes, brought one to Rufe's room at the hotel.

"You cut your hair shorter, but it still looks like you." He wanted to say "especially from the side," but he knew Rufe was touchy about his beak nose, so he said nothing.

But it worried Dan. If the law got Rufe, they would look for *him* nearby, and he had no desire to go back to prison . . . and a gallows.

Rufe decided he would have to shave off his mustache. And when he did so, it changed his appearance a great deal, though it left a pale spot where it had been.

Adele was surprised when she saw him without the mustache. "Why did you do that?"

He told her it was more comfortable without facial hair.

But it was that act that caused her to wonder, and when she finally noticed one of the wanted posters, she began to put two and two together. Her friend was not an iron-goods manufacturer but a bank robber! And he was worth one thousand dollars, dead or alive!

A thousand dollars was a fortune—and it could be her ticket back to Connecticut. She thought about it for several nights as she lay in the dark alone. He was only another trick to her. No man meant anything to her after all the years she had put in at the whore trade. Her sole worry was that he would find out she had turned him in. The poster said he was very dangerous. Would she have to testify in a courtroom with him sitting there?

Who could she ask?

She thought about Charlie Shows. He was a bartender at the Alamo. He had taken her upstairs several times when he was off duty and always seemed like a friendly man. She wandered along to the Alamo Saloon when she knew he was behind the bar. She went before noon when there were few customers. She smiled at Charlie and talked to him alone at the end of the bar where they could not be overheard. She bantered with him for a bit, telling the latest jokes she had heard, at which Charlie laughed heartily —and told her a few. Then she appeared to notice the wanted poster behind the bar and indicated it.

"Would a person turning in a man like that have to testify in court?"

"Naw," Charlie said. "They got all the evidence they need, or he wouldn't be on the poster in the first place." He glanced around and lowered his voice. "Why, you know where Wicker is?"

"Hell, no!" She made a face. "I don't want none of that kinda trouble."

Charlie nodded. "Me neither. He's a killer. You still at the same place, honey?"

"Yeah. Whyn't you come and see me, Charlie . . .?"

"Think I will—in a night'r two."

She patted his cheek and went out.

She did not want to be seen going into the marshal's office. Too many had long memories and sharp tongues. Even the suspicion that she had turned him in could get her killed. She had known owlhooters before, and all in all they were a suspicious, moody, and dangerous lot.

How would she get the information to the marshal? Was he trustworthy? After he had the information would he tell others where he'd gotten it? She had very little intercourse with the law on a genteel basis. She had been arrested many times for being lewd in public places, and the law had not treated her well. She could not trust any lawman very far. If she told the marshal where to find Wicker would he double-cross her and take the thousand dollars for himself?

If he did, what could she do about it? Probably nothing. It would be her word against his, and she was only a common whorelady.

She thought about the problem continually. When she saw Wicker again, he asked her what was on her mind—and she made up some excuse to satisfy him. But that night in bed alone very late, she decided to write the marshal a letter. She would not sign it; she would tell him to reply by putting a letter in the mail basket at the general store, addressed to Robin.

Her letter to him said: If I tell you where Rufus Wicker is, how can I be protected, and how do I know I will get the reward?

Four days later she went into the general store when it

was very busy. She dressed modestly so she would not be stared at, and managed to find the letter in the basket and get out with it. She opened it in her room.

The marshal promised her name would never be made public, she would not have to go into court, and would get the money as soon as Wicker was convicted. However, she would have to reveal her name to the marshal. Nothing could be done if she did not comply.

Adele agonized over that one fact. She was afraid for her life—but she also wanted the money. The thousand would take her to Connecticut and give her some sort of nest egg. She had not been wise with money in the past, but this time, she told herself, it would be different.

She wrote another letter to the marshal, this time telling him where to find Wicker, and telling him her name. He knew her well, of course.

Adele had dithered too long. Rufe Wicker and Dan left the hotel for good the very day she put her letter in the postbox.

The two went to meet the Porter brothers and Phil Bowers. The army payroll robbery was on. Gus had taken a room for them at the Travelers' Home Inn. He had also refined the plan.

"The train will stop for water at a little place called Willows. It's nothing but a couple of houses and the water tank. We'll meet it there, uncouple the express car, and send the rest of the train on its way. It ought to be the easiest job we've ever done."

"Then what?" Rufe asked.

Quinn said, "Then we ride due south for fifty some miles. We divvy the money and separate." Gus had the map on the table and pointed out Willows as Quinn spoke.

His thick finger traced south. "We'll be on the open prairie here, and the law will play hell tracking us, especially when we separate." He smiled round at them. "We can meet again somewhere else—like Kansas City."

Rufe lit a cigar. "No trouble with the express car? Won't the Pinkertons be in it?"

"The Pinkertons take their chances."

Phil Bowers said, "I watched them when they stopped to take on water. There's nothing there at Willows. Like Gus said, a couple shacks, a telegraph shed, and some shirttail kids and dogs. If there's an express car on the train—and there usually is—the trainmen get down to stretch their legs."

Quinn jumped in. "That's when we open up on 'em."

"Ambush?" Dan asked.

"Yes. We can get up close enough to use rifles. Then Phil uncouples the car, and we send the train crew on—"

"What about the telegraph?"

"We cut the wires before the train gets there," Gus said. "We'll also fix it so the engine stops a few miles away so no news gets through to Lyden. It'll give us more escape time."

Quinn said, "So then we blast the express car open and gather up the money." He grinned at them. "And we're all suddenly rich."

"I like the sound of that," Dan said.

Gus poured more drinks. "We'll leave in the morning. Two days to get to Willows, and the train's due the next day." He looked at Rufe. "How d'you feel?"

"I think I'll grow my mustache back."

Chapter Twelve

WALKING Bear was a Kiowa. He was old, dark, and lined. His eyes were dark yellow, the pupils black until he turned into the light; then they were slate gray. He rode bareback with a single cord tied on the horse's lower jaw. He had a silver concha in his black hair. Braids hung in front of his shoulders.

There were eleven men riding with him. The grass was up and they were looking for horses—or whatever they could find. The buffalo were gone, and Walking Bear's heart was heavy, fearing the old days were going fast. There were too many whites coming into the land. The steel rails were crossing the trackless prairie. Why did the whites want his land?

Walking Bear was not a chief; the Kiowas had no chiefs. He was a war leader, a man who could organize a raid and persuade others to follow him. He had heard of horses to the south and had come looking for them. But he had not found them.

However, he had found the rails, with a singing wire beside them on poles. They had halted on coming to the rails, and some of his men had knocked down the wire and coiled it into loops for the copper.

The Indians followed the track eastward as Walking Bear studied the rails. How could he destroy them? It did not seem possible. They were immensely strong and heavy, and he had no tools to attack them. Shooting with a gun did no good at all.

When they came to the water tank, they halted, concealing themselves to study it. Walking Bear could see children playing near the houses. The houses looked very stout, made of heavy timbers with shake roofs and small, square windows. There were no trees.

The tank was close to the rails, a large round affair up on stilts. Walking Bear had no idea what it was . . . but it obviously belonged to the railroad—and it would burn. He was eager to do damage to the hated rails whenever possible.

They would wait until nightfall, he told the others, then they would slip up to the tank and set it afire. When it was burning, the whites in the houses would undoubtedly come out, and they would be able to cut the people down.

The others thought it a very good plan, and they settled down to wait.

To the Indians' surprise, a train came out of the east and halted by the tank. It was a train with only a few cars. The trainmen got down to chat while several men from the houses climbed up on the tank and began to pour water into the train engine.

Walking Bear was not a war leader for nothing. He knew a great opportunity when he saw it. He also knew the men in front on the iron horse were important. He instructed three men to attack them. He and the others of the band would swoop down on the rest.

His plan was perfect for the occasion. None of the trainmen, Pinkertons, or passengers expected an Indian attack this far south. Only a few of those standing alongside the cars were armed.

With terrible whoops and yells the Kiowas charged on galloping horses. The whites were startled, and many froze in astonishment and were cut down by lances and bullets.

The three detailed to account for the engineer and fireman had an easy task: the two died running for the engine. The three braves turned their attention to the men on the tank. One was shot in the chest and fell to the ground. The

70

water poured down wastefully. A second man saved himself by lying flat on top of the tank.

Walking Bear ordered the cars burned, and his men brought brush, piled it under the cars, and set it afire. A few whites jumped off the train on the opposite side and ran off into the brush. The Indians were too busy to follow them.

In minutes the flames licked up the sides of the varnished cars, and very soon the intense heat drove them back.

Walking Bear ordered his men to mount and, with bloody scalps hanging from their belts, the band rode off toward the north. They had obtained no loot, but they had gained much glory. They faded into the prairie, exulting against the hated rails, singing their victory songs.

The train was almost completely destroyed, except for the engine. The express car was ashes; only wheels were left. The eastbound found it the next day and wired ahead for a wrecking crew. The bad news was sent west by a roundabout telegraph to the division point at Lyden.

The newspaper put out an extra, which Gus Porter bought and spread out for them all to see. The goddam Indians had beaten them to the express car.

They would have to wait for another month.

The town marshal at Lyden was named Vernon Stokes. When he received the letter from the whoregirl, Adele, he notified the two Tanner men, and they all converged on the hotel, but Rufus and Dan had flown the coop. When they showed the desk clerks the poster of Rufe, one said he had never seen that particular man, the other said yes, Rufe had lived at the hotel, but he had no mustache.

Neither of the clerks had noticed Laskovy, so probably he had changed his appearance, too.

Marshal Stokes then went to call on Adele. She lived in a room over the Silver Dollar dance hall. He went up the back stairs like an ordinary trick and got her out of bed at ten in the morning.

71

When she opened the door, she was startled, then pulled him inside. "What you want?"

"I want Rufe Wicker. Where is he?"

"He's at the hotel—"

"He left there last night. Where did he go?"

She shook her head. "I dunno. He never told me anything."

"You musta been with him awhile. . . ."

She covered herself with an old robe and sat on the edge of the narrow bed looking up at him. "He told me he was the owner of a factory; then I saw one of those posters and realized who he was."

"You didn't tell him you knew?"

Her eyes opened wide. "Hell, no! I didn't dare say nothing to him. And he never said he was leaving."

It seemed like the truth to Stokes. You could never be sure a whoregirl wasn't lying to you, but this time it sounded all right. She really was scared of Wicker.

And she was probably right. Wicker hadn't told her anything. He said, "If you see 'im again . . ."

She nodded. "Yeah, Marshal. But I don't expect him t'come back if he's gone." Men never came back.

Stokes went back to his office, and the newspaper extra was on his desk. Indians had attacked the westbound at Willow and killed five people and wounded eight more. They had killed the engineer and set the cars afire. Nothing was left except the engine, which didn't burn, and the wheels. It was the worst raid this far south in a decade. The army was sending a troop of cavalry to catch the redskins.

Laredo and Pete Torres came to the office, having heard the news about the train raid. Laredo asked, "Is it possible they were not Indians?"

Stokes was surprised. "Not Indians?"

"It's happened before that whites have raided dressed as Indians."

Stokes shook his head. "I doubt this time. No attempt was made to get into the express car. Whites would have been after the car and probably wouldn't have killed everyone in sight." He grunted. "And scalped them."

"Then it wasn't Rufe Wicker."

"Not this time." Stokes chuckled. "Anyways, Wicker ain't a train robber."

"He knows the Porters. . . ."

"That's so, but where are they?" He told them about his informant without mentioning her name. "She ain't much help because she don't know where Rufe went."

"Damn!" Laredo said.

The next afternoon they learned more about the train raid. It had taken place at a little stop called Yerring. The army payroll for Fort Logan had been on the express car. The gold coins had melted into a heap, and the paper money had been destroyed. The mail had also been burned, and so had everything else in the car.

"The army'll have to send another shipment to pay the troops," Stokes said.

"And they'll keep it under wraps," Laredo replied. "They may even send it by a different route."

After supper they sat in one of the saloons near the hotel, sipping beer and listening to a guitar player who had come in to play and pass the hat.

Laredo said, "We're spinning our wheels now. Should we ask Fleming for another assignment while we wait for Rufe to show himself?"

"There's one thing . . ."

"What?"

Pete rolled a brown cigarette. "Dan Laskovy. Where does he come from? Maybe he's got kin around here somewhere, and the two of them have gone there to hole up."

"Very good idea! Let's wire Fleming in the morning."

They met the telegrapher when he opened his office. The man sent the message, and when the reply finally came, they read it together. Laskovy had been born in Missouri and been sent to jail the first time from there. Fleming could not tell them if the Laskovy family still lived there, north of Joplin. Fleming stated he was making a request to the sheriff of the county and would wire the reply immediately.

It came in several hours. Dan Laskovy had not appeared

in Missouri. The sheriff was positive; he knew Laskovy personally, as did hundred of others. The sheriff was sure he would have heard if Dan Laskovy had shown up . . . because there were plenty who hated the Laskovys and would hurry to do them a bad turn.

"So *that* adds up to nothing," Laredo said. "I vote we go back to talk to Thelma Wicker. She's our only lead."

"It's a long ride to have somebody swear at us. . . ."

"What I have in mind is to get a warrant to search the house. Maybe she's had a letter from Rufe."

Pete nodded. "Pay the hotel bill. I'll get the horses."

Chapter Thirteen

"T HE army will send another batch of money," Gus Porter said, "but our friend at the post won't be able to tell us when it's coming, so we'll have to wait till the next scheduled payment."

Quinn asked, "Why are you so sure they'll keep it secret?"

"Because that's the way they do things." Gus selected a cigar and looked at it critically. "But it'll be worth waiting for. We can still hit it at Willows, which is a hundred miles from where the Indians struck. They won't expect it."

"They might have more guards," Rufe said.

"We'll be told if they do, but I doubt it. They been making the run the same way for years."

Rufe shrugged. "Maybe the Indian raid woke them up."

Gus chuckled. "You're talking about the army. Nothing wakes them up." He lit the cigar. "Quinn and I are going to St. Louis for a few weeks. Whyn't you and Dan come with us?"

Rufe looked at Dan. "Think I'll run down to Texas. What about you, Dan?"

"Figger I'll hit for Pueblo."

Gus nodded. He had a calendar, which he laid on the hotel room table. "The next army shipment comes west on the twenty-fourth of next month, if they keep to the schedule—and no reason they shouldn't. So we all be back here a week before that. Agreed?" He looked round at them. They all nodded.

Rufe did not go back into Lyden. He would have liked one last night with Adele, but if he went back, she would ask a thousand questions—women were like that, weren't they?

His wife, Thelma, would ask enough when he saw her.

It was the end of summer; the weather was still pleasant, the days were hot, the distances shimmered, and the bay horse ate up the miles. Rufe saw no one; there were antelope on the near horizons and prairie hens fluttering away in startled groups.

He came to a settlement the second day, a few shacks scattered here and there with some sheds and tents. He reined in when he saw it in the distance and examined his six-gun and rifle. What the hell were folks doing way the hell out here in the sticks? Evading the law?

He rode in slowly, the rifle across his thighs. Most of the buildings were Nebraska marble, sod bricks with wood-framed windows and plank doors. A few men, gaunt-looking and pinched, stared at him under hat brims. A dark-haired woman peered at him from an open window. A couple of mangy dogs watched him as he halted in front of a door where the word SALOON was printed in grease on a wooden plank.

Rufe got down and took the rifle with him. It was a small room with a ceiling close overhead; it smelled dank inside. The bar was a plank on boxes, and there was a black-belly stove at the back with a black pipe through the roof.

Three men were playing cards at a crude table, and one got up to go behind the bar. "You bring any news?"

Rufe shook his head. "Ain't been anyplace to hear any. You got beer?"

"No beer. Got whiskey and gin is all. Fifty cents a drink."

"Fifty cents!?"

The man shrugged. He was heavyset, wearing a grimy undershirt. He looked as if he'd had a bath about the time the redcoats gave up at Yorktown. He said, "You can go some'eres else."

Rufe sighed, found a half dollar, and laid it on the plank. "Whiskey."

The man poured into a grayish glass and stoppered the bottle. He dropped the coin into a box behind the bar and went back to the card game.

Rufe said, "What d'you call this place?"

"Ain't got a name," the barman said. "You stayin' the night?"

Rufe shook his head. "Reckon I'll move on."

One of the men at the table spoke up. "The good Lord goin' to find you, friend, wherever you is—'cept maybe if you is in Texas. We ain't got a hotel, but you is welcome to sleep in the barn."

"Thanks," Rufe said, sipping the whiskey. "I got to move on." The whiskey tasted awful. He put the glass down, nodded to them, and went out to the bay horse. He would not stay in this godforsaken piece of hell another minute. The air was full of buzzing flies as he rode south, nudging the bay into a run to lose them behind.

It was late in the afternoon, and the horse was walking on its shadow, following a faint track. Was that an outlaw roost he had just left? Maybe they hadn't attacked him because he was well-armed—but they might follow him to catch him napping. . . .

Pausing on a slope, he looked back. He could see the rooflines of two houses. Two men on horses passed between clumps of high brush, headed his way.

Rufe smiled grimly. They were probably after his horse and weapons. They could not know he had near a thousand dollars in his saddlebags. What would they do for a haul like that?

He nudged the horse and went on faster, looking for a spot to hole up, and saw none. He might have to ride all night—after dark he would throw them off by changing course. Did they think him a simple pilgrim? He had seen the elephant and heard the owl. He might even circle and get behind them.

Near dusk he came onto a brushy area and reined in to study it, glancing back. This might do very well. He had left tracks on the ground, but in an hour they would be impossible to see. He got down and led the horse into the thickets.

The brush thinned out after a few yards, and he remounted the bay and rode for near half a mile. Then he got down again, tied the horse securely, took his rifle, and went back. It was very dark now. The moon was not yet out. He walked several hundred yards and halted. This was good enough. He found a patch of grass and lay down full-length, the rifle poked in front of him, the hammer back, ready to fire. He laid the Colt revolver beside it.

And waited.

His ear close to the ground, he heard them some distance off . . . coming closer. Then they stopped, probably to dismount. He could expect them to separate, but not too far, so they would shoot each other. They would come as silently as possible, like lethal shadows. . . .

Rufe smiled to himself. They must be very eager to come into the brush after him. Did they expect to find him rolled in a blanket, asleep?

He cradled the rifle, sliding his finger along the trigger guard. He had selected a spot where he could move the muzzle any direction without obstruction.

Keeping his head still, he moved his eyes, watching for any shadow change—and finally there was one. A lighter form was moving toward him slowly, several yards to his right.

Rufe moved the rifle muzzle with extreme care and sighted on the pale area, probably a shirt. His finger took up the trigger slack as he held his breath.

When the rifle fired, there was a yelp, some threshing, then stillness again, and the acrid smoke slowly dissolved. Rufe laid the rifle down and lifted the pistol, pulling the hammer back as gently as he could, muffling the cylinder sound with his left hand.

His attention centered on the brush to his left, but he

could see or sense no movement. Where was the second man?

He lay perfectly still for perhaps five minutes. Then, his ear close to the ground, he heard hoofbeats far off. They moved away—and it was still.

Rufe smiled. The second man had lost his nerve and had pulled up stakes. He let the hammer down on the Colt and got up. Levering the Winchester, he let the hammer down and moved cautiously to the spot where the man had fallen.

He was dead. The bullet had hit him just above the ear. Rufe turned the body over, a man about thirty-five he guessed, unshaven, with worn clothes and almost nothing in his pockets. A saddle bum trying to better his condition. In the flickering light of a match the deceased looked even worse. He had been carrying an old Starr revolver, and Rufe shook his head in disgust.

He went back to the bay horse, mounted, and continued on south.

Chapter Fourteen

LAREDO and Pete Torres made the long journey to Saylor, navigating by the stars, and only missed the town by a day's ride. They came across a ranch house by a wide, shallow stream, and a man cleaning out a well put them on the trail. They reached Saylor at night, and the next morning were told Thelma Wicker had sold the ranch and gone north.

No one knew where she had gone.

The blacksmith had bought her buckboard and two mules, and had seen her board the stage.

At the stage depot the man in charge told them the stage ran to Newburg, Fairview, and Nevis, about a hundred and fifty miles in all. "They's a spur line of the railroad at Nevis."

Laredo asked, "Could you go east from there?"

"Hell, you could go anywheres from there."

They thanked him and set out. It looked like, Laredo thought, she was going to join her husband. Now that the law knew about their ranch at Saylor, it was no longer a place to hide out.

The man had showed them a map of the stage's route. It made a big swing south to stop at several small towns, so they cut across and came into Fairview in two days. The stage manager in that town told them a woman answering

Thelma's description had been on the stage when it came into town, and was on it when it left.

Laredo had hoped she would get off the stage and rest up in a hotel for a day or two before continuing. But she had not.

They went on to Nevis, arriving there in a day and a half. The woman had left the stage there with her luggage —two small bags. She had gone to The Palace according to a boy who hung around the depot to carry baggage. Laredo gave him a dime, and they went at once to the hotel.

A woman had registered signing herself as Mrs. Robert Wilson. She was in number 17.

Laredo and Pete talked it over. Should they go to her room and force their way in? Or should they wait and see what she did? Maybe Rufe was meeting her.

They decided to wait.

Thelma apparently considered herself far from the eyes of the law. At seven in the evening she came downstairs to supper in the hotel dining room. She had a meal alone, meeting no one. Then she bought a newspaper and went back upstairs. They got a good look at her. She was Thelma Wicker without doubt.

The next morning they followed her to the Pink Slipper dance hall. The front door was closed, but she went around to the alley entrance and went inside.

She was there nearly two hours.

"She knows somebody," Pete said. "Maybe she worked there once."

Laredo nodded. "I wouldn't bet against it. But did she come here just to visit old friends?"

"Maybe she's going to meet Rufe here."

"Yeh. I guess we'll just have to wait and see."

They wired John Fleming, telling him where they were and that they hoped Wicker was meeting his wife. Fleming wired back that he hoped so, too. He also told them the Porter brothers had disappeared from all their old haunts, but he'd had a report they'd been seen in St. Louis. He was checking it out.

Thelma Wicker had been harassed by the law in Giler, and when she returned to the ranch near Saylor, she had been annoyed by men riding across her land, apparently watching her. The local sheriff and his men were not at all sly about their surveillance.

She hooked up the buckboard and rode into Saylor and had a conference with one of the two lawyers in town and had him put the ranch up for sale. It was no good now as a hideout for Rufe. Everyone and his aunt Martha knew about it.

She was sorry to see it go, but ever since the barn had been set afire, she had known it was inevitable. She and Rufe would find another place.

The price she put on the house and acres was low enough that the lawyer found a ready buyer: she suspected he'd bought it himself. She packed up immediately and gave him the address of T.R. Crombe in Nevis—"Send the money to me there."

She sold the buckboard and both mules to the blacksmith and took the stage in Saylor. In Newburg she posted a letter to Henry Whitaker in Fort Griffin, to say she was in Nevis . . . and had sold the ranch at Saylor.

T.R. Crombe owned the Pink Slipper, which was an annex of the Eagle Saloon. Thelma had worked for him for several years before she'd married Rufe. T.R. had been an owlhooter himself in younger days: Rufe had told her that was the way he'd gotten the money to open the Nevis saloon.

T.R. had half a dozen girls working for him in the rooms upstairs and had a large room vacant that he offered to her . . . no strings attached. She moved out of the hotel and prepared to make a stay.

Rufus thought about making a detour to visit Fort Griffin, but the weather was changing, getting colder, and he decided not to. He might easily be caught in a storm or two, which would delay his getting to Saylor.

He was in high spirits as he approached the town. The law would never expect him here, and he would have a week or more with Thelma before returning to Lyden... and this time he would bring her with him. After the job at Willows he would go east with her for a spree. After being alone at the ranch for so long, she would be delighted!

He went around the town and approached the ranch in late afternoon. As he came near he halted at the sounds of hammering. What the hell was that?

He slid off the bay horse at the edge of the trees, took his rifle, and walked forward.

A half-dozen men were putting up a fence around the house! There were two wagons in the yard, one piled high with furniture and the other with goods. He recognized some of the pieces. Somebody was about to loot his house!

Where was Thelma!?

He levered a shell into the Winchester's chamber and strode toward the workers. As he got close he fired a shot into the sky. That got their attention! Everyone halted work and stared at him.

Rufe growled, "Who the hell's in charge here?" He moved the rifle muzzle along the line of men.

A voice from the house said, "I am." A dapper-looking man came off the porch and walked across the yard toward him. "Who are you, sir?"

"I own this property," Rufe snarled, centering the rifle muzzle on the lawyerish-looking man.

"Are you Mr. Wicker, sir?"

Rufe glowered, then nodded slowly. He pulled the hammer back. "Where's my wife?"

"She's gone. I don't know where, Mr. Wicker. She did not tell me." The man held both hands up, then slowly pulled a folded paper from an inside pocket. "This is a deed, sir. Your wife sold this property to me." He offered it, and Rufe stepped forward and took it.

The man said, "I am a lawyer, and that paper is in order.

83

The money has been sent to Mrs. Wicker in Nevis."

Rufe read the paper and stared at the prissy man. In Nevis! That meant T.R. The lawyer confirmed it.

"I sent the money in care of a Mr. Crombe."

Rufe handed the paper back and let the hammer down on the Winchester. So she had sold the ranch! He glanced at the workmen, who still stood waiting, at the house, and at the lawyer. Well, the place was no hideout any longer. He could never stay here in peace. . . .

He grunted and turned, walking back to his horse.

As he rode away he could hear them hammering again. Thelma was a surprising woman. He never did know what she was thinking. . . .

He rode into Saylor and left the horse at the livery to be rubbed down and fed. Then he had a meal, with people staring at him—did they know how much he was worth? He bought a cheap tablet and an envelope and wrote a letter to Thelma in care of T.R. Crombe telling her he was in Saylor on his way to Lyden. He would write to her from there.

People stood in doorways watching him walk to the stable. He posted the letter and rode out, ignoring them. How many of them were worth a thousand dollars?

He looked at the sky. It was overcast and the air smelled like rain.

Chapter Fifteen

THELMA received Rufe's letter informing her he was heading for Lyden. She was annoyed, but probably he had business there. She knew he and the Porters were thick. Rufe was not a letter writer and said very little in the single page.

She had received the money from the lawyer, and with what Rufe had given her she had a tidy sum. Thinking it over, she decided to go to Lyden.

She packed her bags, bought a stageline ticket, and got on the Concord one chilly morning as a light rain was falling.

It took forever to get to Lyden; a bridge was out, and they had to make a long detour; the rain became a deluge for an hour one day, and the roads were impassable; it took four days to get to the town.

Thelma put up at the first hotel she came to. Where was Rufe? He had not said in the letter. She had not realized Lyden was such a large town. How would she start looking for him?

Finally she went to the weekly and put a note in the Agony column: THELMA KOLBE IN TOWN FROM SAYLOR, TEXAS. SHE IS STAYING AT THE HANOVER HOTEL.

If Rufe read the paper, his eye might be caught by her maiden name—or the name Saylor. It was all she could think of. But it brought results. A boy brought her an envelope. It was from Rufe. He was astonished she was in town. He was staying at the Travelers' Home Inn under the name Robert Winters. He asked her to come there.

She went at once, and Rufe met her at the door. "What the hell are you doing here?"

"That's a nice greeting!"

He hustled her to a chair in a corner of the lobby. "We're about ready to go on a job! I'm leaving in three days. Why didn't you stay in Nevis?"

She pouted. "I wanted to be with my husband."

"But you can't—we're planning a big one—I ain't got time for anything else. Why don't you go back to Nevis, and I'll meet you there after this is over. It ain't safe here."

"Nobody's after me."

"But you might draw 'em to me. I don't go out in the daytime—this town is full of posters."

Thelma sighed. There was much in what he said. He had told her often enough the law would hang him if they caught him. She said, "Why can't I stay here till you get back? Nobody knows me as Kolbe."

"But Nevis is safer for both of us. Nobody knows about T.R.—"

"That lawyer does. He sent the money to T.R."

"Who is he goin' to tell?"

She almost cried. "But it's cold and miserable on the stagecoach. It's raining out, Rufe!"

He finally relented. But he insisted she go back to stay at the Hanover Hotel. He would see her when he could.

Gus and Quinn Porter were back from St. Louis, and Phil Bowers showed up the same day as Dan Laskovy. They were together again in the Porter suite, looking at the map Gus spread out.

"Here's what we'll do. We hit the train at Willows. The payroll will be on it, according to our friend at Fort Logan, just like always. We uncouple the engine and the cars and send 'em on—"

"Why do that?" Dan asked.

"To get rid of 'em," Gus said. "But before we get to

Willows, we'll pile rocks on the tracks a couple miles down so they have to stop, and we'll cut the telegraph lines. Then we can blow the door off'n the express car, takin' our time." He looked round at them. "Understand?"

They nodded.

"All right. Then we put the payroll in bags and head south." His finger traced the route. "We go here to Curry's Mill. It's a little burg in the middle of nowhere. We split up there. Me and Quinn is going back to St. Louis." He looked at Rufe.

Dan said, "I'm going back to Pueblo."

"Think I'll go out to Omaha," Phil Bowers said.

Rufe shook his head. "I'll think on it."

"All right. Get your possibles together tonight. We'll leave after breakfast." He rolled up the map.

That night Rufe went to the Hanover and up to Thelma's room. With the door locked he said, "We're ridin' out in the morning. And it won't be smart f'me to come back here. I'll meet you in Nevis."

"Then can we go to New Orleans?"

He nodded. "We c'n go anywheres."

"How much will you get?"

"I dunno, but it ought to be sizable."

He left the hotel before midnight and rode back to the Travelers' Home Inn. This was the first time he had ever depended on another man to do the thinking on a job as big as this one. Dan Laskovy usually let him do the planning when they hit banks. So far it had paid off well.

Well, Gus seemed to know what he was doing—and he and Quinn had done it before many times. So they probably knew the pitfalls. . . .

Rufe was up at first light and got his few possessions together and met the others in the dining room. They had all settled their bills the night before. . . .

Gus had brought along a heavy steel lever, and while the rest of them piled rocks between the rails, Gus pried spikes out of the ties. If the train crew managed to halt the engine before hitting the piled rocks, and got out and removed them, they might not notice the spikes removed farther along—and thus derail the train.

Quinn and Dan fired at the insulators on the poles and brought down the telegraph wires, coiling lengths of them and tossing them into the brush a distance from the rails. It would be impossible for the telegraphers at any station to know where the wires were down. Repair crews would have to be sent out from each end.

Then they went on to Willows, reaching it at dusk. The train with the express car was due at 8 P.M. There would be only a lone telegrapher and the people in the two houses to deal with. Since the wires were down, the telegrapher would probably be in one of the houses—and he was.

They came up on the blind side of the houses and quickly rounded up all of them, two men, including the telegrapher, one older boy, three kids, and two women. They were herded into a small windowless room.

"Nobody gets hurt," Gus told them, "if you-all stay put."

The telegrapher's shack was near the water tower, and they crowded into it to wait. It seemed a very long time before they heard, far across the flats, the rumble of the engine, and the whistle sounded for Willows.

Rufe felt himself tense and tried to relax. This was a lot different from walking into a bank. He watched as the headlight came into view, the engine slowed as brakes squealed, and the cab was enveloped in the biting odor of steam and coal smoke.

There was the engine and coal car, four passenger cars, the express car, and the caboose. Rufe and the others quickly ran out: Dan to the engine, his revolver holding the engineer and fireman in the cab; Quinn and Phil to the cars, and Rufe and Gus to the express car.

Three men came out of the express car, and Gus quickly lined them up while Rufe disarmed them. Phil uncoupled the express car, and in a moment the train moved out, leaving the two cars behind. It went like clockwork.

Gus turned to the prisoners. "Who's in the express car?"

"Three men," one said.

Gus nodded. "You three, get moving." He pointed with the revolver. "Down the tracks. Follow the train."

They hurried.

"Where's the dynamite?"

"Here," Phil said. He showed two sticks.

Gus took the sticks and moved to the express car door. He shouted, "You inside—come out, or we dynamite the door."

There was no answer.

Dan said, "They probably don't believe you."

Gus smiled grimly. "They will in a minute." He pushed one stick into a crack by the door, then looked around at them. "You-all better get behind something. . . ."

A muffled voice from inside yelled, "Let's talk about this."

"You had your chance," Gus yelled back; he lit the fuse and ran to the telegrapher's shack. As he reached it the explosion came. It knocked him down, and the concussion rocked the shack.

Gus picked himself up, and they all hurried back to the car. Phil and Quinn had lanterns. They held them up to show the end of the car had been shattered. A gaping hole yawned where the connecting door had been. Smoke eddied and curled away. Gus, with Rufe at his heels, entered the car. The three Pinkertons were sprawled at the far end like so many rag dolls—all of them out cold. Rufe took their weapons and examined them as Quinn held a lantern high. The three were cut and bruised but alive; they might be woozy for days.

The payroll was not in a safe but piled in neat wooden boxes with government seals. Quinn broke one open. It was filled with carefully wrapped bills and gold coins.

"We's rich," he said, grinning.

It was a lot to carry. Dan pointed out the two mules in a corral by the houses. "We can use them to pack it. . . ."

They found wooden trees and quickly loaded the treasure onto the mules. Then they headed south in high spirits, bantering with one another, discussing ways to spend the loot. . . .

The law would play hell catching them, Rufe thought. The telegraph lines linked only towns on the railroad, and to send information to other towns required a rider or a stagecoach, and by the time the news arrived, it might be very stale. Rewards would be offered, of course, and bounty hunters might seek their trail—but probably not if they thought a gang were involved. A bounty hunter could get perforated as easily as any other citizen. Also railroad detectives were tenacious. They would put names and descriptions on the wires to everywhere.

Official investigations, however, had a way of dying out rather quickly. The law had too many other problems.

Rufe, Dan, and their friends rode south to Curry's Mill, as Gus had pointed out. It was really in the middle of nowhere. It was one single log-and-stone house and a few sheds and a corral. Curry must have hauled the logs and stones many miles. Rufe could see no indication why it was called a mill.

Curry was a big, whiskered man with a thundering voice. His wife was an Indian, and there were five or six kids and as many mongrel dogs running about. Curry demanded news, and Gus told him they had just heard the railroad had been held up.

Curry laughed and invited them in for a drink.

The stone house was not nearly large enough to hold all the Currys and dogs and the five unexpected visitors, so they camped outside by a wash where a trickle of water flowed and pooled, several hundred yards from the house in a fringe of dusty trees.

They waited till the lights went out in the house, then by the light of a low fire they split up the money in the sacks. Gus divided it, working slowly as they all watched him intently. There was not quite as much in the payroll as they had expected. Each man received a trifle over ten thousand dollars, most of it in greenbacks.

They all grumbled when it was totaled. Gus said ten thousand for not much work wasn't bad. Rufe shoved his lot into the saddlebags. He had gone into banks and come out with less. . . .

But all in all, he thought, banks might be the best bet. Rufe lay awake for a long time, his head on the saddle. He and Dan could go into a bank alone and what they got was theirs. They didn't have to share with three other men.

It took a lot less planning. And maybe a lot fewer men on their trail afterward. The army was sure to raise hell.

With a bank the getaway was the main thing—losing a posse or covering a trail. . . .

Well, he was ten thousand richer. In the morning he would hit for Nevis to see Thelma again. Then they could go to New Orleans as they had planned.

Of course it would be nice to spend a week with Klara first. . . .

Chapter Sixteen

THELMA Wicker took the stage, buying a ticket to Lyden.

They watched her go. "She finally got a message from Rufe," Pete said. "He must be in Lyden."

"Or in that area." Laredo frowned as the stage disappeared in the distance. "Unless . . ."

"Unless what?"

"Unless she knows we're watching her, and she'd leading us away from Rufe."

"She doesn't know who we are."

"She's seen us once, close up. If we turned up here, she'd be very suspicious. How do we know whether or not she has seen us here and we weren't aware of it?"

"Ummm. Possible. Not terribly probable."

Laredo shrugged. "Well, we haven't any choice. We'll have to follow her. Let's settle up and wire John Fleming."

"All right."

They went across country, not following the stage road, and it took five days to arrive in Lyden. And several more to locate Thelma Wicker. She was under an assumed name. If Wicker and Laskovy were in town, they, too, were under other names . . . and so were the Porter Brothers.

Then they heard about the robbery and murders at Willows. The local paper was full of it. Reporters had a field day describing the incident, and a sketch artist had drawn the scene, imagining the robbery in progress.

The two men who had died were Pinkertons. They had been inside the car when the dynamite explosion had blasted the door open. Survivors described several of the robbers, and Rufe Wicker was high on the list. When shown the wanted sheet of Wicker, they all identified him. There had been five men in the gang. The telegrapher, Hosea Simmons, was the best witness. He described the five and had heard one call the other Rufe and another Phil.

"It fits," Laredo said. "Rufe and Laskovy, the Porters and Phil Bowers."

The telegrapher had seen the five ride off to the west, toward Lyden. But it was very unlikely they had returned there.

A wire came from John Fleming concerning the Porter brothers. Informants had said the Porters were in the habit of returning east, to one of the large cities, after a particularly big or satisfying job, to celebrate. They were big spenders in every regard: easy come, easy go.

Fleming was certain that after the Willows payroll heist the Porters would head for the east . . . maybe with Wicker and Dan Laskovy. His order was: Track them down!

There was no tracker in Lyden, and the old-timers they talked to in the saloons told them the chances were the only good trackers were under contract to the army.

Besides, the trail was cold. Since the incident at Willows there had been fitful rains; tracks were washed out. There was no telling which way the group had gone. They might have split up. Using a map, Pete pointed out a railroad about a hundred miles from Willows. "They might have gone to that."

There was also a stageline about fifty miles north. "Give or take a few. They might have gone either way—if they were heading east."

Laredo looked at the map thoughtfully. "There's one other option."

"What?"

"The fifth member, Phil Bowers. Let's ask Fleming what they have on him. It may lead us to something else."

"Good idea."

Fleming's report, when they received it, was thorough. Bowers was thirty-four, unmarried, and had been born in Omaha, where he still had many relatives. He was just out of prison, serving time for armed robbery. The case against him had been poor in evidence, and he had been let out early.

"Omaha," Laredo said. "A man just out of prison pulls another robbery with the Porters and is on the run. Would he go home?"

"He might. He might have relatives who would hide him."

Laredo bent over the map. "We're here, and Omaha's here." He moved his finger across the map. "A good journey on nothing but a hunch."

Pete said, "Our lives are made up of hunches. I think he would go home instead of going east with the Porters . . . if the Porters go east."

"What if he went somewhere with Rufe and Laskovy?"

"That plays hell with my hunch."

"Yes, but I think your hunch has a good solid maybe mixed into it." Laredo folded the map. "Let's go to Omaha."

Thelma Wicker enjoyed her stay in Nevis, waiting for Rufe to join her . . . until she overheard Dora, the fluffy blonde. Not knowing Thelma was nearby, Dora was recalling various fun escapades with "Wicky." She had met him first a few days before his marriage in Denver, and had been seeing him off and on afterward for two years.

Thelma had heard hundreds of tales from whoregirls over the years and would not have listened to this one a moment except for the mention of Denver and the pet name "Wicky."

She stepped into the doorway and faced the girl, Dora. "Who are you talking about?"

Dora was instantly defensive. "None of your damn business!"

Thelma advanced on the other and pulled a derringer. "Tell me, you little bitch!" She heard the other girls in the room scurrying to get out of the line of fire, and someone yelled for a bouncer. They were upstairs in the girls' crib rooms.

Dora began to cry. "I never done nothing—he came to

me with money. What the hell, Thelma—I didn't know he was your husband . . . not at first!"

Thelma took a long breath. Neither Dora nor any of the girls would have refused money. . . . She put the gun away and turned her back as one of the bouncers came charging into the room. "Who's got the gun!"

"Nobody," Thelma said, and pushed her way past him.

She went to her room and locked the door behind her. She had always known Rufe was no lily-white, but she had thought he loved her. She had given up the whore trade for him. Had never been with another man since their marriage in Denver. And the Lord knew she'd had plenty of opportunities.

It was as if someone had punched her in the stomach, for her to listen to Dora's account of the two of them in a hotel room . . . only a day before the marriage! She did not for a moment doubt Dora's tale. Dora was not creative enough to make up anything.

She gave herself over to a spate of crying as she lay on the bed. Dora had inferred that she had come to Nevis expecting to meet Rufe here. He had written to her then.

How many others had he written to—had he bedded? Where exactly was he now?

He would never tell her. She knew how he hated questions. Now she knew the reason. The sonofabitch was leading a double life!

She moved back to the hotel that evening when the girls were all occupied. She could no longer bear their chattering and gossip. Now, she knew, they would gossip and chatter about *her*. They had a new topic to discuss endlessly. And the insipid blonde, Dora, would be in the middle of it, adding spice.

The weekly newspaper featured a story about the train holdup at Willows, with the speculation that it was the work of the Porter gang and Rufe Wicker. Descriptions fitted them.

The robbers had gotten away with an army payroll worth thousands—the exact figure was not given. Two men had died of wounds, and five others had been hurt or wounded. The reward for Rufe Wicker had been raised to twelve hundred dollars . . . dead or alive.

The Pinkerton Organization that had employed the agents who were killed was offering an additional five hundred dollars for each of the robbers . . . in any condition at all.

The newspaper contained a drawing of the Porter brothers and a photograph of Rufe and one of Dan Laskovy.

Thelma wadded up the paper and threw it across the room.

A day later T.R. Crombe sent a boy to her with a note. The note informed her Rufe was in town, that he did not want to be on the streets in daylight, and asked her to come to the Pink Slipper, where he would meet her in a back room.

Thelma went at once.

The dance hall was closed. It did not open till evening on weekdays. Thelma stood in front of the saloon doors and took several deep breaths. Then, gritting her teeth, she pushed the bat-wings aside and entered.

It took a moment for her eyes to adjust to the dimness. She could hear murmurs and the click of pool balls off to the right. But her eyes were fastened on the man at the end of the bar. Rufe wasn't in one of the back rooms at all. He was standing at the bar with two others, laughing at something one of them had said.

No one seemed to notice her for a moment. But as she began to walk toward Rufe the room quieted. She saw Rufe look around, and in that moment she pulled the derringer.

She pointed it and drew back the hammer. Her finger tightened on the trigger as she heard Rufe yell. She saw the men scatter as the gun fired.

She saw Rufe whip out a pistol . . . and nothing more.

"Jesus!" Rufe said in a hushed voice. "She was tryin' to shoot me!" He slid the Colt back in his belt. Someone knelt by Thelma, felt her pulse, and looked up at him, shaking his head.

T.R. appeared. "What happened?" Someone told him, and he took Rufe's arm. "Come outa here—come on—one of you men, go for Doc Penny." He pulled Rufe into his office. Rufe slumped into a chair.

"She was tryin' to shoot me!" He was in shock. "She was gonna shoot me!"

"We've got to get you outa town," T.R. said urgently. "She's dead, you know."

Rufe nodded dumbly.

"Why'd she want to kill you?"

Rufe shook his head. "I got no idea."

"You two been quarreling?"

"No, course not." Rufe took a long breath. "Where the hell will I go?"

"You got to be damned careful, Rufe. There's posters with your picture on 'em everywhere."

Rufe nodded. "Why the hell she want to shoot me?" He looked at T.R. almost helplessly. "We was going to New Orleans soon's I got here."

"Maybe she didn't want to go."

"Hell, no, she was crazy to go . . . after me for a long time. That wasn't it. . . ."

"You got to get out tonight, Rufe. There's no place I can hide you. They'll search this here—probably the first place they'll look."

"Yeah, all right. . . . You got a drink, T.R.?"

The other put out a bottle and two glasses. "Don't tell me where you're going. . . . But you go somewhere good, and stay outa sight for a spell. Can you do that?"

He thought of Peevy. "Yeah . . ." He downed the liquor and sighed deeply. "Goddammit, T.R., why'd she want to shoot me?"

Chapter Seventeen

IT would be a long ride to Omaha. Laredo estimated it to be something like three hundred and fifty miles, give or take twenty or thirty. There was no stageline that went that way; it was possible to go directly east to the Missouri River and take a steamboat upstream . . . but in the end they decided to go across country. They bought a pack mule to carry supplies, and set out.

For days they saw no one at all. The prairie was a vast sea of grass. Their only companion was the wind. At night the stars hung at their fingertips, and an occasional drizzle let them know winter was on its way. There were a few settlements, hardly to be called towns, shacks, and tents set down haphazardly, lonely as leaves floating on a wide pond.

But Omaha, when they reached it, was a city, and a division point on the Union Pacific Railroad. The city sprawled along the broad valley of the Missouri and onto the high bluffs beyond. Laredo and Pete walked the horses through the unpaved streets, surprised to see so many shops with German names. Men lounged in doorways and watched them go by. Where would they start to look for Phil Bowers?

The city had several newspapers, and they discussed putting an ad in them, but Bowers would probably be suspicious of that. He was undoubtedly here in secret, so who would know to place an ad . . . no matter what it said?

There were dozens of saloons where he might hang out—a saloon was a man's club, after all. But it might take months to visit them all . . . and then find nothing.

They put up at the Riverside Hotel and bought newspapers to read over supper. On the front page of each paper was the poster photograph of Rufus Wicker! He had just shot and killed his wife in a town called Nevis!

"Santa Maria!" Pete said in astonishment.

Laredo read the item. It said Thelma Wicker had entered a saloon in Nevis where Rufe, her husband, was drinking with friends. She had taken a derringer from her purse and fired at him. Rufus had instantly drawn and fired back—and killed her. His companions had said later it had been a purely reflex action on Wicker's part. He had drawn and fired, hardly realizing the woman was his wife.

T.R. Crombe, owner of the Pink Slipper saloon and dance hall, where the shooting took place, described himself as shocked to learn the desperado, Rufus Wicker, had been in his establishment.

Rufus Wicker had apparently taken to his heels at once according to the local police. No one knew where he had gone. The police further stated they had found more than five thousand dollars hidden in Mrs. Wicker's hotel room. They theorized this money was probably part of Wicker's loot from robberies, and it was impounded.

"I'll be damned," Laredo said. "He shot his wife!"

Pete frowned at the newsprint. "Why did she try to shoot him?" He sighed. "I s'pose we'll never know."

"And now he's on the run. . . ." Laredo folded the paper and put it aside. "He'll probably hole up somewhere for a while till the noise dies down. Do we have any posters left?"

"Not many. But he'll never come here to Omaha, will he?"

"I doubt it. How do we start looking for Bowers?"

"This is a bigger town than I thought." Pete shook his head. "We haven't a single lead. He's not long out of prison, so they may have photographed him. . . ."

"But it'll take weeks for us to get the photo through Fleming and have posters printed and handed around. He could be long gone from here by then. Maybe we'd better track down all the people named Bowers in town. Fleming said he had relatives here."

"Yes. But it'll be tricky."

It was also difficult to find people named Bowers. There was no central listing of names. The local law knew of several families who had had minor scrapes, and gave them directions.

The first family they visited lived on the edge of town, near the river. They looked the house over from a distance. There was a well-worn wagon parked in front on the dusty street, and an older man rocking on the porch.

They watched the curtains on the windows as they approached, and they did not move. The old man did not get out of his chair but shouted at them that he knew no Phil Bowers. A stout woman came to the door and looked at them curiously.

"He's not here," Pete said.

They went to the next house, farther out of town, near the railroad tracks. A youngish woman told them she had three kids, none named Philip. "Are you the law?"

Laredo shook his head, but she closed the door on them.

When they rode to the end of the street, Laredo looked back in time to see a small boy run from the house. The boy crossed the tracks and ran across a brown field.

"Let's see where he goes," Laredo said.

They followed the boy from a distance and watched him enter a cluster of shacks. Pete looked at the sun. "He's in there somewhere. It'll be dark in four, five hours. . . ."

"He could be gone by then."

"It's a chance we gotta take. . . ."

They returned to the hotel and went back to the shacks after dark. As they came close they saw there was a row of houses, weather-beaten shacks, all connected, facing other smaller shacks, a corral, and a stable at the rear. Bowers could be in any one of the five houses in the row, or the three smaller ones. A few people were sitting outside the doors, chatting and smoking.

Leaving the horses, Laredo and Pete separated. Pete went down the row behind the houses, to the stable. Laredo walked to the first people outside and asked them where he could find the Bowers family.

As he, a stranger, appeared, the chatter stopped, and they stared at him. Then someone said, "No Bowers here."

Laredo took a step—then a shot was fired. It came from somewhere near the stable, and a second shot followed. Laredo drew his Colt and ran that way, hearing sudden hoofbeats.

Then five shots sounded close together as someone emptied a six-gun. There were confused sounds as Laredo reached the front of the stable building, and Pete appeared, shoving shells into his pistol.

He said, "I think it was Bowers. He fired at me as he galloped past. I think I hit the horse."

He led the way along a dark path, and after forty or fifty feet they came onto a downed animal. The rider had been thrown off and was unconscious on the ground. Pete took the man's gun and tied his feet.

Laredo scratched a match and looked at the horse. Pete had hit the animal with four shots and killed it instantly. The man had been lucky; he had not been touched, but the fall had knocked him out.

He said, "It's Bowers, all right. There's a PB burned into the saddle."

Pete struck another match and peered at the fallen man. "He matches the description." He rolled the man over and tied his hands behind him.

Several people appeared, and Laredo walked toward them. "Go home; this is police business."

They muttered, but the word *police* had its effect, and they shuffled away, talking among themselves. Pete had Bowers on his feet, still dazed, but able to walk. They took him back to their horses, put him up behind Pete, and rode back to the city. He said nothing at all.

At the first police station they came to they took Bowers

inside and identified themselves. Bowers still refused to talk, but a sergeant said they would round up some relatives to name him in the morning. He was locked up, and they returned to the hotel.

The arrest did them little good. Bowers steadfastly refused to talk. He was quickly identified and finally admitted being Phil Bowers, but denied being with the Porter brothers and others at the Willows robbery.

However, a large amount of money was found in the saddlebags of the downed horse, money Bowers could not explain.

"Where the hell is Nevis?" Laredo said, frowning at a map. "Maybe Oklahoma Territory?"

"Or Kansas. . . . Here it is." Pete put a finger on it. "Down near the Texas border. Dead south of here." He rolled a brown cigarette. "But Wicker won't be in Nevis."

"Where will he be?"

"He could be in the next room for all we know." Pete scratched a match and blew smoke at the ceiling. "You decided he'd hole up somewhere, remember?"

Laredo grunted. "I still think that's his best bet. But it's no good for us. Let's wire Fleming and ask for a list of his early pals. Maybe one of them is keeping him out of sight."

"Could be a woman, too."

They walked to the nearest telegraph office and sent the coded wire. The reply came in five hours, delivered by a boy to the hotel. Fleming wrote that not too many of Rufe's early pals were still alive. Banditry had a way of weeding them out. But he had been able to list a few, and of those he could not be positive all were alive. And he had no idea of their whereabouts.

At the top of the list was a man named Jonah P. Velie. His nickname was Peevy, according to the old-timers, and he had been in the owlhoot trade most of his adult life and had been a known confederate of Wicker when he was active.

Another name was Kid Ransom, all that was known of

the name, and Fleming wrote there was a possibility he had been fatally shot in a holdup in middle Texas. At least the description tallied, and there had been nothing heard from the Kid since.

A third name was Victor Arn, alias Adams, alias Agen. He was a cattle rustler but had been known to run with Wicker years ago.

"Never heard of any of them," Laredo said, pulling his chin. "What's your suggestion?"

Pete frowned and fingered the telegram sheets. "We know Wicker hung around Longworth and Giler. What if we went back there to ask about these names?"

Laredo nodded. "Good idea. Let's do it."

They returned to the police station before leaving town. A sergeant took them aside. Phil Bowers had done a bit of talking, he told them. "We got a room down in the basement. You can't hear a thing from it."

"You beat him up?"

The sergeant made a face. "We sort of persuaded him to talk. Some of the boys worked him over, but they ain't a mark on him that will show in court."

"What did he say?"

"He was at the Willows holdup, all right. The two Porter brothers and Wicker and Laskovy was there, too. They run south and split the take and separated. He don't know where the others went. He thinks the Porters went east."

The police were wiring the sheriff of Lyden County, and Bowers would be sent back there to stand trial for robbery and murder.

"That's one of 'em," Pete said.

Chapter Eighteen

RUFE Wicker hurried from the saloon to the livery and saddled his horse. A woman shot, no matter who she had been, was exciting news that would flash from one end of the town to the other like summer lightning.

He got off the main street and cut across back lots and was out of town in minutes, heading west. He had no idea where he was going, but he knew the news would go out on the telegraph: Rufe Wicker had shot and killed his wife!

He hadn't known it was Thelma till his finger had pulled the trigger. As the shot fired he recognized her. She had come into the saloon with the light behind her; she had been only a female form . . . for a brief second, and he had fired only because she had.

But no jury in the land would listen to his explanations. He had shot a woman—and his wife at that—and they would hang him. He was too damned quick with a gun.

Well, he would shed no tears for Thelma—why she had come to kill him was a mystery. But of course there were other women, and this time he would not marry one of them. When a woman got that ring on her finger, she became possessive. Thelma had shown it in little things. . . .

He was certain he had hidden his escapades with whore-girls from her. They would not talk out of turn, so it must have been something else. He had always been generous with money—when he had it. He had given her a good amount of the bank money . . . what the hell had made her shoot at him?

He shook off the wonderings. Where should he go?

He thought about Peevy . . . and the smells of the house. But Peevy was his best chance. Only Dan Laskovy knew about him. And Dan would never talk. He would have to put up with the smells for a time, till the hullabaloo died down. Another exciting news story would come along and drive Thelma's shooting out of people's minds. The sheriffs would shuffle his wanted sheet to the bottom of the pile. . . .

Miles from the town he turned south toward Longworth. He would stay out on the trackless prairie and navigate by the stars. It was safer to avoid folks; those damned posters were everywhere. Dan Laskovy had found it easier to change his appearance. But he, Wicker, had too-definite features. By now probably any sheriff in the land would recognize him on sight. It was one hell of a heavy cross.

He missed Longworth but came across a stage road and followed it on a guess, and it led him eventually to the town at dusk. He circled the town and rode on toward Peevy's place in the hills. Several miles out of town he halted and rolled in his blankets for the night, telling himself this was the last time for a while. The weather was turning cold.

In the morning he continued and arrived at the house as a light rain had begun to fall. Peevy was astonished to see him. "You know all the law in this goddam country is lookin' for you!"

"You been readin' the papers again?"

"Hell, ever'body talkin' about it. Why you shoot Thelma anyway? Come on in outa the rain."

Rufe stripped the saddle, bridle, and blanket off the horse and carried them into the house. It smelled the same. Peevy had a fire going, and he went over and warmed his hands.

Peevy said, "Well . . . ?"

"Well, what?"

"Why'd you shoot Thelma?"

Rufe glared at the other. "I didn't know it was her. She came in shootin' at me—what the hell I going to do?"

"Why she shootin' at you?"

"I ain't got any idea. You goddam nosy, ain't you?"

Peevy grinned at him, exposing toothless gums. "When it's all over the papers, it ain't just your business anymore. She find out you running around with other women?"

"What makes you think I runnin' around with other women?"

"Hell, you allus did." Peevy poked the logs in the fire. "Papers also sayin' you and the Porter boys robbed a train."

"You sure read a lot of papers, old man."

"What the hell else I got to do? I too old to chase women."

Rufus sighed. He had to put up with the smells *and* with Peevy. It might be a long winter.

It was a long, weary ride to Longworth, and it rained half the time. They avoided Lichfield and rode into Longworth at midday. The skies had been clear the last day and a half, but it was cold as a polar bear's butt when they got down in front of the local lawman's office.

The law was town marshal Jim Duttin, who had been appointed only that week. Before that he had served a hitch in the cavalry. He was a dark, dour-looking man who nodded over their credentials. "Who you looking for?"

"Rufe Wicker."

Duttin grunted. "Two bounty hunters by here a day or so ago. They lookin' for him, too. He's worth twelve hunnerd dollars, any way they can get him."

"He used to hang out here. . . ." Laredo smiled. "That's what they tell us."

"Yeh, I heard that, too. Before my time."

Laredo said, "Lemme try three names on you, Victor Arn, Kid Ransom, and a man called Peevy."

Duttin frowned. He shook his head. "Never heard any of them."

But the general store owner had. "Peevy? Hell, he comes in here ever' month—sometimes sooner. He got him a place out in the hills some'ere's. I never been there. Think he said it was a day's ride, something like that."

"But you don't know which direction?"

"No, I never been there, like I said."

Pete asked, "What's he like, this Peevy?"

"Old man, hops around on a wooden leg. Closemouthed old coot. There's talk he was an owlhoot once. That's how come he got the leg."

"When was the last time he came into town?"

"Well, the last time he come in here was . . . lessee, maybe two weeks ago." The storekeeper was curious. "What you want him for? You lawmen?"

Laredo smiled. "We don't want him for anything. Just like to ask him some questions."

They went to the hotel and signed for rooms. The hotel had an outhouse with a large copper tub for twenty-five cents a bath. They took turns in the tub, then went down the street to supper. Pete said, "I got a hunch we're getting close to Wicker. Peevy's place sounds exactly like what Wicker would want at this particular time when his picture is in all the papers."

Laredo nodded. "A day's ride from here . . . in which direction?"

They finished a supper of steaks, pie, and coffee and went back to the hotel. The latest weeklies were in from Giler. Rufe Wicker's picture was no longer featured. Someone had robbed a stage and been recognized, and the story pushed Wicker to the middle pages. And that item said only that the reward for Wicker was now twelve hundred dollars, dead or alive.

In the morning they wired John Fleming to tell him where they were and what they expected. Fleming's reply said that the Porter brothers were definitely in St. Louis— they had been seen there, and army authorities were trying to get their hands on Phil Bowers, charging him with murder and grand larceny. Bowers's future was certain.

Fleming had no advice for them concerning Wicker,

other than to stay with it. He had no news of Dan Laskovy.

They could find no one else in town who knew—or would tell them—about Wicker. The general feeling seemed to be that Wicker should not have shot his wife, even though she had thrown down on him. It was felt she would have missed him with both bullets in her over and under, and that in general it was a bad policy to reduce the number of females in a land starved for the same. Wicker had been too damned quick to shoot.

The storekeeper had told them Peevy was a close-mouthed old coot, and he was apparently right. No one they talked to knew anything much about him. No one had bothered to see where he went when he left town in his old buckboard. There were a lot of old coots around. Peevy didn't stand out, except for his wooden leg. Many men had wooden legs from the war, but Peevy was the only one who came to Longworth.

He had given it out he'd received the wound that caused his leg to be lopped off in the service of Bob Lee. But Fleming's report said it had been shot off by an outraged citizen when Peevy tried to rob him.

There were three roads out of town. One led into the undulating prairie; the other two led into low hills. It was likely Peevy's home was in the hills. But where? In a saloon they talked to several men who had hunted the hills. One said, "They's places back in there where nobody's ever been."

"Could you hide a cabin or a house there?"

"Hell, you could hide yourself a goddam castle in there. They's caves, too. You could live in one o' them caves. Nice sandy bottoms . . ."

Peevy had to live where he could take a wagon. And a wagon meant tracks. If he'd lived there a long time, Pete said, and come into town once or twice a month, he might have made a road somebody could follow.

"We could go look," Laredo said. "We might get lucky."

It was a misty morning when they set out. They flipped a coin to decide which road to follow. They passed a number of shacky houses set far back from the road. Dogs barked at them and dull-eyed cattle stared from brown fields.

Past noon they had seen no turnoff roads and had come to low brushy hills. Pausing by a muddy creek where driftwood was beginning to pile up on the curves, Laredo indicated the road stretching away from them.

"It's skirting the hills, not going into them. What d'you think?"

"We may have picked the wrong road."

"Maybe Peevy takes a different way into town every time, to keep from making ruts."

Pete rolled a cigarette and nodded. "We'd better go back and start again."

It was raining softly when they returned to town, and lights were coming on along the main street. They put the horses in the stable and had supper. By full dark the rain was coming down in torrents.

It rained all night and all the next day before it began to taper off. Muddy water rushed down a deep gulley in the middle of the main street. People put planks over it to get across, and the saloons closed early for lack of customers.

The next day the weather cleared, but there was water everywhere, in puddles, in small streams, in soggy earth. Too much water. They decided to put off the exploration for another day. Let the sun dry things out.

That afternoon a wind came up out of the west and stayed for supper, battering the sides of homes and buildings and dying down in the night. It accomplished more than the sun in drying the land.

In the morning Laredo and Pete set out once more, taking the second road leading toward the brown hills in the distance.

They found the road to be a quagmire, and most often rode near it. Swift running water had cut deep ruts across it in many places. By the middle of the morning they were into the hills, winding through shallow valleys. The road curved back and forth, never straight, following the valleys.

However, this road or trail soon petered out, dividing

into half a dozen barely visible paths wandering off in various directions.

They could see no recent wagon-wheel marks or ruts. Pete thought the rain would have effectively erased any. "There's too many choices," he said. "It'll take us weeks to run them all down—unless we're lucky as hell. How far do these hills stretch?"

"From the map I'd say twenty or thirty miles. We're just on the edge."

"And we're looking for one little hideout cabin?"

Laredo sighed. "You figure we should wait for Peevy to make his next trip into town?"

Pete got out the makin's. "It's the surest bet." He glanced around them. "We may be in the wrong part of the hills."

"All right. Let's go back."

Chapter Nineteen

IT was with a certain satisfaction that Rufe Wicker received a note from Dan Laskovy, routed through Henry Whitaker in Fort Griffin. Dan was en route from Pueblo to Peevy's place. It seemed Dan had come home to find Beatrice in bed with another citizen, and Dan had perforated the citizen and beat up the girl. She had then informed the law that a certain owlhoot was inhabiting her precincts. Dan had been forced to go out a back window and steal a horse.

He was understandably annoyed at the circumstances, especially at her, since they had talked about roses and cottages. But she had reverted to type—which he had been afraid of from the beginning.

It did not occur to him she had felt somewhat the same way concerning his profession.

The letter preceded him by four days because he had stayed over in a small railroad town; he still had money to spend and let it be known to several comely saloon girls who were eager to lighten his load.

Rufe was restless and thinking of bolting when Dan showed up. The smells and the solitude were getting to him, he told Dan.

"Did you see any of those damned posters on the way here?"

"No. Never saw one. It's been a little while." Dan

looked tired but professed himself ready to go—after a few good nights' sleep. "You got anything in mind?"

Rufe had not. He had started to grow a beard, which itched abominably. Peevy assured him the itching would stop when the hair grew out a little. Dan thought it would change his appearance considerably.

The two men walked away from the house to talk. Rufe had been impressed by how easy the holdup had been at Willows. "We ain't got any inside information about payrolls, but we could sure as hell go through a passenger car and fill a few sacks."

"Pick up what we can?"

"Sure, whatever they got on 'em."

Dan made a face. "That means we got a sack'r two full of watches and jewelry and odds 'n ends. Where we going to sell it?"

"There must be places. Besides, there'll be money. Folks traveling got to have money with 'em."

"Jewelry got names on it."

"They can be filed off. You in or not?"

"Hell, I'm in, but this ain't the same as going into a bank. You figger two of us can handle it?"

"Why not? One goes down the line collecting goods, and the other one stands guard at the end of the car. Folks'll be looking into the barrel of a gun."

Dan rubbed his chin. "How'll we get away?"

"I been thinking about that. We could stop the train by piling rocks on the track. Then we'll have the horses right there. But we'd need another man to be outside while we're inside."

"But if we don't . . . ?"

"Then we'd have to wait till the train stops—or we jump off."

"Jumping off could mean a broken leg."

"Then the next thing is to get on the train and ride it to some little whistle-stop where we'll already have horses waiting."

Dan shook his head moodily. "Jesus, that calls for a

week's work before we even get on the goddam train. Maybe we better find another man."

"Yeah, I about figgered that, too."

"You think this's easier than going into a bank?"

Rufe grunted. "We ain't even tried it yet. I mean the two of us. It might go easier than you think."

"What about Peevy for the outside man?"

"Naw." Rufe fished for a cigar. "He's too goddam old and stove up. Besides, he'd forget what the hell we was there for."

As they walked back to the house a light rain began to fall. That night the storm hit, and it rained for three days. Winter was on them.

When it cleared up, Peevy waited two days so the sun would soak up the water, then hit for town in the old buckboard to buy supplies. When he returned, he had the latest weeklies.

Rufe and Dan read them with gathering frowns. Phil Bowers had stood trial in Lyden, and a jury had convicted him of train robbing and murder. They had hanged him behind the courthouse, and someone from Omaha had claimed the body.

Peevy also had some disturbing news. The general storekeeper had told him two men had been asking about Rufe Wicker.

"He figgered they was law."

"Did he tell them where we are?"

Peevy grinned toothlessly. "He don't know."

"Somebody could follow you."

"Nobody has. Besides, I never go the same way twice."

Rufe and Dan talked about it away from the old man. The two men in the general store had probably been bounty hunters, Rufe thought. He had had a deal of experience with those kinds. In his opinion they were as big thieves and murderers as the worst badmen on the wanted sheets. They would backshoot without warning.

Dan thought it was to be expected that bounty hunters were asking about them in Longworth. "They probably asking about us in every town."

113

"Yeh . . . maybe so. . . ."

To Rufe it seemed the world was closing in. There was always the specter that one day they would grab him and he would dangle at the end of a rope. Why had Thelma shot at him? Had some bounty hunter convinced her he was worth more to her dead than alive? But he had given her money—thousands!

Maybe she had spent it all. . . . But he would have given her more if she had asked for it. Hadn't she known that?

He ought to leave here and go south, into Texas. To hell with robbing a train. He still had money in his kick. Now he had to think about his neck!

Dan did not oppose the idea. He was not sleeping nights, he said. He worried every time they went outside that someone was drawing a bead on them. Besides, he told Rufe, the smells were getting to him, too.

The weather was clear and cold, a good time to travel, if one had to travel in winter. They settled with Peevy, warned him about talking, to which he glared at them, saying he was not an old woman, and set out in the gray light of dawn.

Laredo and Pete learned a day or two after he had left that Peevy had been in town. He had come for supplies, the storekeeper said, as he always did. He did not know if Peevy had stayed overnight. He had been driving a mule and his old buckboard as usual.

Pete suggested they try to follow his tracks. The ground was still soft, and the buckboard's wheels would cut deep, and they would be fresh. How many wagons would head into the hills?

They only found one. And it was surprisingly easy to track. No attempt at all had been made to conceal the wagon ruts. The pair followed them into the hills in a winding, almost wandering path that led eventually to a wood-and-stone house where smoke rose from the chimney.

They observed the house from a distance with binoculars. There was a corral with two mules, the buckboard

114

drawn up beside it, and nothing else. No horses.

Laredo said, "I think they've flown the coop."

"If they were ever here."

"Lets's wait a bit and see if anyone comes out. They may have left the horses somewhere else . . . But I doubt it."

"Let's circle the house; see if there's another door."

"Good idea."

But there was not. The several windows were small and high up. Two had glass; the others were boarded up. After they had watched for several hours, a limping man came from the house, went to the ricked-up wood beside it, and carried in several armfuls.

"That's Peevy," Laredo said. "He's got a wooden leg."

"And he's alone."

"Let's holler the house. The door is the only way in or out. What you say?"

Pete nodded. He slid his rifle from the scabbard on the horse, jacked a cartridge into the chamber, and lay down on the grass, centering the front sight on the door.

Laredo yelled at the house.

Nothing happened for a few minutes. He yelled again, and the door opened a crack. Peevy yelled back. "What you want?"

"Come on out."

"Go to hell."

Laredo nodded to Pete, who fired a round, and splinters jumped off the door just above where Peevy's head would be.

Peevy yelped. "What the hell you shootin' at me for?"

"Come out and talk."

The door opened reluctantly, and Peevy showed himself, both hands up. "You got no call to be shootin' at innocent folks!"

"Are you Peevy?"

The old man admitted it. "I ain't wanted for nothing."

"Are you alone in the house?"

"Course I am!"

"Walk on down here."

Peevy stumped away from the house, eyeing Laredo. "You the law?"

Peevy was unarmed. Laredo told him to put his arms down. "Stand right there where we can see you." He indicated Pete. Peevy nodded, and Laredo walked to the house, the Colt ready.

The door was wide open, and no one was inside. He stepped in, holding his nose, and backed out again. It smelled like a mule had died there some time ago. He went back to Peevy. "Where's Wicker?"

"Where's who?"

Laredo said, "Make it easy on yourself. You want to go to jail, we will accommodate you."

"Jail!? I ain't done nothing!"

"You've hidden and aided a criminal, Rufe Wicker. You can go to jail a long time for that."

The old man's voice was high-pitched. "You can't prove nothing!"

"We can put you in jail on suspicion."

Pete towered over the little man, and his voice turned harsh. "Let's beat it out of him."

"Wait a minute, Emilio—" Laredo pushed between them. "This old man doesn't want a beating—"

"Who cares what he wants?"

"Git him away from me!" Peevy was terrified.

"He's going to talk." Laredo pushed Pete away. "Don't hurt him. . . ." He faced Peevy. "Tell us about Wicker."

Peevy edged away from Pete. "Yeh, he was here, him and the other one, Laskovy. They lit out two days ago."

"Where to?"

"I dunno. Rufe talked about going to Texas. . . ."

"Where in Texas?"

The old man almost wrung his hands. "I dunno! They never told me nothing! They went out in the woods there talkin' among theirselves. They never said nothing in front of me."

That sounded like truth, Laredo thought. They probably were careful what they said in front of the old man. Pete agreed. Owlhoots like Wicker and Laskovy were not stupid.

They left Peevy in the house and walked the horses south, following tracks that might have been left by the two outlaws. Pete said, "Where's he going in Texas?"

"I was about to ask you."

Pete sighed and dug out the makin's.

Chapter Twenty

THEY headed for Fort Smith on the Arkansas. Rufe thought they might find some entertainment there. They both had money burning their pockets, and a little diversion was due them.

Rufe's beard was thick and dark, a little too long for comfort. Peevy hadn't owned a pair of scissors, and he had been forced to cut it with a knife, not a very practical arrangement. It had left him looking very ragged. But as camouflage it was excellent.

The weather did not improve. A series of rain flurries drove them inside when they came to Fredail, a small town on a stage road. They left the horses at the livery and put up at the small hotel beside the stage station. It rained for two days, a steady downpour that delayed the stage-coaches. Bridges were out on the streams and telegraph lines down.

Rufus spent much time in the saloons and in the Lone Star met Rose. She was an attractive girl who was impressed by his talk and his ready cash. He told her he was a cattleman on the way south after selling a herd.

She was on her way east with several other women. They had been forced to stop over because of the impossible condition of the roads. It was fate, Rose said, they had met in this little out-of-the-way town. She was a saloon entertainer, she told him: she sang and danced for a living.

He paid her for the time she spent with him in her room on the second floor, a large room crowded with walnut furniture and muslin curtains on the two windows.

They spent most of the time together in bed. Rufe smoked black cheroots and told her lies about his ranch in Texas.

One night he put the cigar in a dish to embrace her, and the cheroot rolled out of the dish onto a carelessly dropped newspaper.

The two did not notice the fire until it was licking up the wall, consuming the curtains in seconds. The heat caused Rufe to glance around; then he yelled and scrambled out of bed to dash the basin water on the flames. It did no good at all. Rose screamed, grabbed her clothes, and ran into the hall stark-naked.

Rufe spent several minutes slapping at the fire, but it spread in both directions; the wallpaper was dry as tinder. He grabbed up his clothes, shoved into his pants, and ran.

Rose had awakened the second floor. When she ran downstairs into the saloon, she caused a sensation. One of the bartenders threw a blanket around her as she screamed her alarm. The house was on fire!

Fire was the most feared calamity in any wooden town. There was a volunteer fire group that could be called together on ringing a firebell. But no one remembered the bell in the sudden excitement. People were streaming down the stairs from the second floor, most of them yelling at the tops of their voices.

It was very late: the rest of the town was asleep. The only water was in the horse troughs along the street, and it was a pitiful drop. . . . By the time everyone was in the street, the saloon was a torch, and the flames were spreading northward as the wind suddenly seemed to gust, pushing the flames along.

Rufe got his clothes on—he had no idea where Rose had gotten to. Dan Laskovy appeared, with their saddlebags, and they ran to the stable for their horses. In quick sentences Rufe explained what had happened. He had definitely caused the fire, and if Rose happened to mention that fact to the townspeople, they might very well come after him with a length of rope. Many would lose everything. . . .

The conflagration seemed to be gaining in strength as building after building took fire. Rufe and Dan slipped out of town, heading south. It was certain the entire town would go up in smoke.

Seventy miles south they stopped in Galesburg and heard the news from the telegraph. Fredail had been almost totally destroyed. Only the buildings south of the saloon had survived the fire. It had even jumped the street and taken out five buildings there.

What Rufe feared had happened: Rose had talked. She had dashed naked into the saloon and had later been questioned. She admitted she had had a customer in her bed, and described Rufe. He had called himself Luke Wilson. He had started the fire with a careless cigar. Wilson, she said, was a wealthy Texas cattleman.

Rufe groaned. Someone had drawn a sketch of him from her description, and it was much too accurate, gracing the front page of the newspaper. He shaved the beard at once.

The death of a town was a calamity and was thus reported in all the newspapers west of St. Louis. Laredo and Pete Torres, halted by the rainstorm, were in Caleb, a small crossroads burg where the weekly from the county seat was delivered every Thursday.

"Luke Wilson," Laredo said, gazing at the sketch. "He ought to be more imaginative."

"He didn't know then that he was going to burn down the town. The name was just for this Rose person."

"Well, it pinpoints him. I wonder if Laskovy is with him. The paper doesn't say."

"He must have gotten out while the fire was still burning."

"Yes, and he's heading south. Fredail is pretty far south of Longworth anyway. Is he going to Texas?"

Pete nodded. "Looks that way. What's for him in Texas?"

"Lots of questions," Laredo said. "Damn few answers. Maybe he wants to get away from folks like us."

"Yeh. We must have put out three-thousand wanted sheets. Maybe he's been seeing his face everywhere he looks."

"I hope so. Let's get moving. . . ."

They talked to a bartender who said he had been to Fredail. There was no road from Caleb running directly there. "You c'n take a set at it," the man said, "'cross country. Keep a-bending left—not too much, and you ought to wind up pretty close."

"Vague," Laredo said when they went out to the horses. "A hell of a lot of guesswork in this country and no road signs. If we miss Fredail, we could wind up on the banks of the Red River."

"One thing: Rufe will know the story will be in all the papers. He might guess we'd solve the name: Luke Wilson. So he'll be gone up the flue."

"You think he might head east instead of south?"

Pete shrugged. "I would if it were me."

"But you have a college education."

"That's so." Pete grinned. "I ought to show Rufe Wicker my diploma."

"When we catch him."

The weather held fair as they moved across the trackless prairie. It was cold, but the rain did not come. They came across an occasional huddle of warped-roof buildings, usually set alongside a stream. A few people stared at them as they approached and passed, and once someone fired a rifle, the bullet whanging over their heads.

Laredo merely waved in reply. What the hell were folks doing out in the middle of nowhere?

"They want to be let alone," Pete said. Probably as good an answer as any. They might have law problems or disagreements with a church. . . .

In two days they spread out, barely in sight of each other, to cover as much territory as possible. But still they missed the town. They had been bending left as the bartender had suggested, and maybe too much left. They both estimated they had come far enough, so they turned west . . . and ran onto the town in another day.

There was little left of it, perhaps a dozen buildings and shacks. The wind had come from the south that night and had blown the flames along the street. Nothing north of the once-saloon had survived. There had been five deaths— laid to Rufe Wicker's door. People were bitter.

Although rebuilding had started, the town would never be the same. Too many could not afford to rebuild, and some had already left.

They talked to Hugh Billings, who had owned the saloon where the fire had started. He was a potbellied man with white hair. "We put that gal, Rose, on the first stage. Told her t'get the hell outa this part of the country. Don't know where she went." He blew out his breath. "Don't give a goddam."

"What about Rufe Wicker . . . ?"

"Only saw 'im once. Called hisself Wilson. Spent all his time with Rose, far's I know."

"Was there another man with him?"

"I never saw 'im if there was, but Charlie at the livery says they was two. You talk t'him."

The livery stable was one of the few buildings that had not been burned. Charlie, the owner, was a weedy man with a pipe stuck in his face. Yes, there had been another man with Wicker, he confirmed. He hadn't got a good look at him, though. . . .

Pete described Laskovy, and Charlie nodded. "That sounds like him." The two had galloped off to the south about the time Charlie had noticed the fire. No one had followed the two men, everyone being busy fighting the raging flames.

Laredo said, "So they could have gone in any direction after leaving here."

"Nearest town is south," Charlie said, "forty, fifty miles."

Laredo looked at Pete. "Then we may as well go there
. . . see what we can find."

Pete nodded.

They looked the horses over for brush cuts, stone
bruises, saddle galls, and sore mouths, rubbed them down,
and had Charlie feed them the best oats after he examined
their shoes.

They set out at dawn after a night in the stable. There
was a road of sorts between the two towns, and they made
good time with the wind behind them and rode into the
burg, called Nally, in the middle of the evening. The only
hotel had seven rooms, five empty. "Take your choice,
gents. . . ."

Laredo showed the clerk a wanted sheet with Rufe's
picture and the man frowned at it, put on his specs, and
held it out, studying it. "Seems like I seen him. . . ."

"Lately?"

The man sighed. "I just ain't sure."

"There was another man with him," Pete said. He described Laskovy.

"He might have shaved the mustache," Laredo remarked. "You might remember his big nose."

The clerk said, "He maybe never come in here. I just
ain't sure. Course Ronnie Lee is on duty half the time. . . ."
He pointed toward the back. "He's sleepin' now."

They went down the street to a restaurant, then up to
their rooms. Ronnie Lee still hadn't come on duty.

But he was behind the littered desk when they came
downstairs in the morning. He proved to be a little round
man with hair fluffing about his ears, steel-rimmed specs,
and an eager manner. He glanced at the wanted sheet and
nodded quickly.

"Yes, I seen him." He rubbed his nose. "Only, something's different . . . not sure what. . . ."

"Was there someone with him?"

Ronnie Lee nodded again. "Never got a good look at the
second feller, though. Only seen him once. Them two
didn't mess with folks much. Stayed by theirselves."

He had no idea where they had gone.

Laredo and Pete consulted the map tacked to a wall of the telegraph office. It concentrated on telegraph lines and repair roads and was more than five years old, the telegrapher told them. But things hadn't changed much.

The nearest town south was some eighty miles, but there were closer towns, one of which was Ruxhall, the largest. It was southeast, and the telegraph wire and road went directly there.

"How large is Ruxhall?" Laredo asked.

"Oh, that's a big place." The telegrapher took off his green eyeshade and rubbed his eyes. "Must be five thousand anyway. Busy town. That's horse-and-cattle country, you know. Man can find almost anything in a town that size. Of course it's not New Orleans. . . ."

They thanked him and went out to the boardwalk. Pete fished out the sack and began to roll a cigarette. "Big place," he said. "A man can find anything in a town that size."

"That's what he said."

"Can you think of anyone a big town might attract?"

Laredo smiled. "I think so."

"I think so, too."

Chapter Twenty-one

FRED Canfield had been a stagecoach driver for six years, until a Pinkerton man had come snooping around. There had been half a dozen stage holdups in a year, and the owners of the stageline were beginning to get suspicious of their own employees.

It seemed to them an employee was giving the holdup men information about shipments. How else would the gang know which stage to hit and which to let go by?

The undercover investigation wound down to two people finally: Fred Canfield and a woman in the office. Real evidence against them was tentative, but when both were let go, the holdups stopped.

The woman got on a train and went east. Canfield became a bounty hunter.

In his hotel room in Ruxhall he shuffled through the stack of wanted sheets he had accumulated and set one aside. Rufe Wicker was worth twelve hundred dollars dead or alive. He was said to be in this neck of the woods. He was dangerous as a teased sidewinder, but the money was good. It was worth a little risk. Of course there were ways of shooting a man without much risk attached. . . . Canfield liked the "dead or alive" ones: it gave him a certain leeway. He knew what people said about the position of bulletholes in the bodies he brought in, but he got his money and was gone. To hell with them.

He read all the newspapers he could find, carefully. Newspapers were full of interesting information to a man in his line of work. For instance, Rufe Wicker had been behind the fire in Fredail—not too far away. The chances were good he would come to Ruxhall. If only for the girls. Canfield had learned that owlhoots like Wicker lived it up when they had it, because it was easy to get more, and none of them expected to live forever. Like some people.

So he frequented the saloons, examining the patrons, especially those who avoided the brighter lights. One night he spotted the man coming down the back stairs of the Star. The man had been up in the crib rooms; he came down now, got a mug of beer at the bar, and took a chair near the far wall away from the hanging lanterns.

Canfield watched him sit down and light a cigar, then he walked past the man slowly. Jesus! It *was* Wicker! He would swear it on a stack of morocco-bound Bibles. He walked past and got a beer from the bar, to sit twenty feet away where he could keep Wicker in view without seeming to.

Twelve hundred dollars was sitting there—so close!

Wicker took his time finishing the beer, then got up and went out. Canfield followed him to the street and watched him go into the hotel.

How would he take this man? Wicker was certainly armed and wary as hell. It would be foolish to face him. Canfield considered himself a good man with a gun, but Wicker was probably better. His notoriety said so anyway. It was only a guess as to how many men he had killed. Some thought twenty. And he had certainly faced some good gunfighters in his time. According to the newspaper stories, he had shot and killed his own wife when she came into a saloon and fired at him. A witness said, according to the news items, Wicker had drawn and fired so fast he hadn't realized the woman was his wife.

The second day Canfield kept Wicker under surveillance he realized there was another man with him—it must be Dan Laskovy. The newspapers had mentioned him often as a killer. Worse and worse. Canfield wanted no part of two experienced gunfighters.

He would have to down Wicker with a rifle from a distance. At a time when Laskovy was not with him.

But when he killed Wicker, would Laskovy come after him? It was something to think about. In order to claim the bounty, he would have to identify himself as the killer. And that information was then public knowledge.

Maybe he should shoot Laskovy first. . . .

There was also a bounty on Laskovy of one thousand dollars, which he might be able to collect after he shot Wicker. He had dreams of collecting from both. More than two thousand dollars! He had never had that much money at one time in his life.

But he had to be damned careful in shooting either one of them.

Neither Wicker nor Laskovy seemed to have any plans about leaving town, though Canfield knew they were capable of leaving at a moment's notice, being used to fast exits.

They had no particular pattern to their movements; they went to the restaurants, not always the same one, and they spent much time in the saloons, as did all men. They were frequently together, but not always.

Neither of them lingered on the streets.

After watching them for four days trying to decide his best course, Canfield was aware Wicker walked from the hotel to the nearest saloon every day, never at the same hour and always in the afternoons.

Across the dusty street and roughly between the hotel and saloon was a barn belonging to the Hay-Grain and Feed store. Canfield looked it over and found it a not too difficult matter to climb to the roof of the barn from behind it. He could then walk on a narrow but flat surface to the front of the building where there was a five-foot-high false front running the width of the barn.

It was an excellent spot; he could rest a rifle on the parapet and view the entire street. He would have a good shot at Wicker, and it might be hard to tell where the shot came from, a thing much to be desired, since he had to climb down again.

Canfield, standing behind the parapet, watched Wicker walk from the hotel to the saloon, and rubbed his hands in satisfaction. Wicker would be an easy target.

That night he cleaned his Winchester and reloaded it. He should need only one shot. If Laskovy showed up, he would point the man out to the local law.

As he saw it, his plan had only one drawback: he would have to spend time, maybe hours, on the roof of the barn, keeping the boardwalk in view. Anyone might spot him by glancing up . . . and wonder what a man was doing up there. It was chance he would have to take.

Canfield slept fitfully that night, dreaming about missing Wicker with his first shot and facing a fusillade from the outlaw's gun.

He stayed in bed late, telling himself he was resting. When he went out to breakfast, he carried the Winchester. That caused no comment—many men toted rifles even in town for one reason or another. A man did not ask another man his business.

As midday passed he went around to the back of the barn and climbed to the roof.

Ruxhall was a big place—three times the size of the little burgs they had been in lately. It even had two hotels, and they signed for rooms at the largest, which had three floors. Laredo's room had a polished wood dressing table with a rather cheap gilt mirror. The carpet had recently been renewed and was a deep green color, which did not set well with the wallpaper.

But the bed was firm, and the white water pitcher was new, though the yellowed curtains had been through a great deal and were thinking ahead to retirement. Pete was across the hall, their horses in the stable behind the hotel.

Laredo wired John Fleming immediately, telling him where they were and what they suspicioned. Fleming's return wire said the Porter brothers had left St. Louis and were presumed on the way back to Lyden or another likely town, and were probably broke. Fleming suggested they would be looking for a way to refill their pockets. Maybe they would contact Wicker and Laskovy to help in that regard.

The Senate Saloon was next door to the hotel, a room of brass and gilt fixtures and chandeliers, with two pool tables and huge paintings of interesting-looking women on the walls. Laredo and Pete sat at a table with beer mugs in front of them, listening to the click of pool balls and the constant murmur of voices.

"We'll have to make a tour of the line houses and probably the saloons," Laredo said. "Wicker's biggest weakness is women."

"He's got a lot of weaknesses."

"Well, let's concentrate on this one."

Pete lit a brown cigarette. "Saloon girls are terrible liars. . . ."

"True." Laredo sighed. Across the room several painted girls were laughing with a gathering of cowboys. Those women used different names, perhaps for every client, and nothing they said could be taken for truth unless checked. As Pete inferred, going that route to gain information about Wicker might be laborious.

It had to be done, and the sooner they got started the better.

Finishing the beer, they went outside; it was late in the afternoon, a dreary day. There was a ring around the sun, a sign of rain. The line, a string of brothels, was to their left, on the edge of town, and they turned that way.

As they approached the Hay-Grain and Feed store Laredo saw the sudden bloom of smoke from the roof of the barn and in the next instant heard the shot.

Someone had fired into the street! Pete had also seen the smoke, and they started running toward the barn. The shot had been fired away from them, but Laredo could see no one hit.

He ducked into the narrow space between the barn and the next building, with Pete pounding at his heels. Somebody had bushwhacked another citizen, a very reprehensible thing to do. A man liked to have an even chance. . . . He saw a fast-moving figure drop to the ground and disappear almost instantly. The figure had been carrying a rifle, but it happened too fast to get a shot off.

When he got to the spot, no one was in sight. He told Pete what he'd seen, and they made a search. The barn backed up to an alley where there were a dozen or more sheds and privies, and a few small corrals. There were also wagons and carts, hundreds of places for a pursued man to hide.

They found nothing. To Laredo's surprise, nobody from the street came around the barn to look with them. Apparently no one suspected the shot had come from the barn roof.

When they returned to the street, there was no crowd and no downed man. A few shopkeepers stood in doorways, and Laredo asked one what had happened. The man shook his head, saying he'd heard a shot but maybe it had been fired into the air. "Usually happens on Saturday night. . . ."

Rufe Wicker was a lucky man, but then he was not one to walk along a street with his eyes on the ground . . . as many did. He had learned years before that he had to be alert while in public. It had saved his bacon before—and it saved it now.

He caught a flash of sunlight reflected from something —a gun barrel? It was on the roof of the feed store barn. Not a place for an ordinary spectator to be. Rufe ducked into a doorway as the shot came, splintering the wood beside him.

Snaking out his pistol, he looked around the corner at the roof, but no one was there. He saw two men run to the barn and into the space between it and the next building. He did not follow.

Who the hell had shot at him? Too damned many people were shooting at him lately. Even Thelma had . . . He sighed. Probably a bounty hunter had either tracked him here or had recognized him. Maybe he should grow the beard again. . . .

Dan Laskovy was asleep in the hotel room. When Rufe woke him and told him what had happened, Dan said without hesitation, "Bounty hunter. Somebody seen one of them damn posters and recognized you."

Probably that was it.

"We got to travel," Dan said. "Only way we can keep them off our backs is to keep moving." He found a cigar and lit it. "If he was on the roof, then that means he was waitin' for you."

"I already figgered that out. He knews we's here in the hotel. Probably knows about you."

"I reckon. So best we slide out tonight. How's your money?"

"Gettin' low," Rufe said. "Wonder if them Porters is still in St. Louie. . . ."

"I d'want to hit no train. Let's us find a nice quiet bank like that one in Ruskin. Maybe we ought to go back and hit'er again. Will they expect that?"

Rufe shrugged. "Maybe not, but it's a far piece from here. Lots of banks in between."

Rufe hated to go, but it was safer. The unknown sniper would doubtless strike again if he had an opening. They paid the bill and took the road south as soon as it was full dark.

Chapter Twenty-two

BOTH hotels—the town had only two—were between them and the line houses. Laredo hauled out and unfolded the well-creased wanted sheet. They showed it to both clerks, and one nodded. "Think he was here. . . . He left last night." He opened the register and ran his finger down a list of names. "Called himself Winters. His friend was named Tasker."

The clerk had no idea, of course, where the two were headed. "I wasn't on duty when they left, but they paid the bill some time after supper."

"They left after dark," Pete said. "So they probably took the road."

"North or south?"

"You want me to guess? South."

They passed oxen carts creeping along on ungreased, squeaking wheels, a high-loaded wain, and several buckboards, all coming into town. Among the sheds on the outskirts of town were several log buildings with skeleton roofs covered with canvas. Cottonwoods decorated a creek. Then they were on the prairie again with a high sky where buzzards circled, busy making a living. The clouds had disappeared, and for a day the weather was brisk with hardly any wind.

By late afternoon they were in a region of jumbled low hills and trees. The road, such as it was, snaked in and about the slopes, trying to remain on a level but not succeeding too well. Laredo wondered if Wicker knew this country? Was he headed somewhere in particular?

Pete thought he might well be keeping on the move. After all, they had gone after other badmen in their time who had done the same thing. It seemed to be characteristic of the breed. It was definitely harder to get a moving target in one's sights. Owlhoots were something like Indians, too: it was impossible to outguess them.

When the road branched, they halted and frowned at the tracks—or lack of them. The ground was hard and had dried out. Which way had the pursued taken? The right-hand path led on toward Texas; the other went east.

"Flip a coin?" Laredo said.

"I think we ought to look for sign. You go one way, I'll go the other for a few miles." He glanced at the sky. "We can meet back here in two hours."

"All right. Good idea. What if they haven't taken either road?"

"Today we guess; tomorrow we weep."

"I didn't know you were so poetic."

Pete sighed and took the path to the right.

Laredo took the path to the left, walking the horse, watching the ground. It had been a long chase after Wicker and Laskovy, and not over yet. Both sides had had some luck, but had it run out for him and Pete? Taking this road had been a guess. Wicker could easily have cut across the dark prairie and be miles away by now.

He and Laskovy might have backtracked, too, and be heading north instead of south. Laredo shook his head in annoyance. Too damned many maybes.

He came to a patch of damp earth, where thick trees shaded the ground. Across the earth were horse prints—two horses side by side. He got down and looked closer, fingering the earth. Probably made only a few hours before.

Wicker and Laskovy?

He drew his pistol, opened the loading gate, and turned the cylinder, looking at the brass, then reholstered it. He pulled the Winchester from the saddle boot, levered a cartridge into the chamber, and let the hammer down.

Mounting, he peered at the trail ahead, the rifle across his thighs. The road—or trail—led in and around the slopes where trees and brush grew in profusion. He could not see more than fifty yards in any direction.

But then, neither could they.

Should he go back for Pete? He probably should, but the tracks were there, plain on the ground, and they pulled him along. He looked at the sky. An hour or so till dark. Maybe they would stop and make camp. Probably they had no idea they were being followed.

At each turn he stopped to listen, then went on. A light breeze rustled the dry leaves of the trees around him, and the small leather squeaks of the saddle seemed louder than usual.

The slope suddenly changed as he rounded a hill. In ages past there had been a mountain slide. It looked as if a giant knife had sliced away the hill and piled up dirt in careless heaps at its foot. Trees grew there now, and the path led through the jumbled earth.

It was necessary to cross a short stretch where nothing grew but brown grass and weeds. Halfway across this a pistol shot shattered the near silence. Laredo thought he felt the wind of it on his cheek.

He had expected to see a horseman, but the man firing at him was afoot. The man fired again and again, too fast.

Laredo turned, galloping for the trees to his left. He'd had a quick glimpse of a man afoot who had dropped the wood he'd been gathering, and yanked out his pistol. It had looked like Wicker.

He gained the shelter of the trees. No more shots followed him. Wicker and Laskovy were probably about to make a camp, and Wicker had been gathering wood for a fire.

Damn! Laredo swore under his breath. They were prickly as hell—well, they were owlhoots, likely to fire on anyone who came on them suddenly.

He slid down, tied the horse and, taking the rifle,

moved toward the spot where he'd seen the shooter. If it was Wicker and Laskovy, they might try to ambush him or they might run—not knowing if they'd seen the point man of a posse. Probably they would hightail it, figuring to lose anyone who followed in the dark.

Laredo moved cautiously and in a dozen minutes came on a place where the man, if it had been Wicker, had punched out brass and reloaded the revolver.

He had not picked up the wood he'd dropped. Laredo went on more quickly; in a few moments he found where the two had halted. But they were gone.

They could not be more than minutes ahead.

Would Pete hear the revolver shots? Maybe. He debated for a second of two. If he went back for Pete, an hour might pass—and it would be black night. If he went on, he might catch up to them—he might. It was a chance worth taking.

It never once occurred to him he would be one to their two.

With the butt of the rifle resting on his thigh, he rode on, wary as an Apache. It was not yet dark, but the shadows were gathering fast, and it was getting colder. The trail was poorly marked, and he worried he might ride off it and lose precious time finding it again.

Would they ambush him?

Probably not. Shooting in the dark was guesswork and . . . they would not know if one man or twelve would shoot back.

The thing that worried him most of all was that they might not follow the trail—such as it was—but cut off at an angle into the wilds. They could ride a hundred yards off the trail and wait for him to pass, or they could keep going, and he would never find them. Not until daylight let him discover tracks.

Lady Luck was ignoring him this night. As someone had once said, "Bad luck is more prevalent than good."

When it came full dark, he halted, unable to see the trail. Now he should go back for Pete—but he could not.

The trail had turned and twisted, and he would be lost in moments in the darkness.

With resignation he moved to one side, finding a flat area, and settled down to wait for sunup.

Pete Torres followed the trail, moving at a walk, looking for tracks, and found none at all. The trail had been much used in the past, but any tracks were long gone, washed out by rain and wind.

He went on till the shadows began to close in, then, looking at the sky, he decided he had an hour of daylight left. He turned about and rode back to the junction of the two trails. Laredo was not there.

He waited only a few moments, then took the left trail. He came to the same wet patch of ground, in the fading light, and made the same assumptions as had Laredo. Two men had passed that way, but were they Wicker and Laskovy?

When darkness closed in, he halted and got down to wait.

Rufe Wicker dropped the firewood and whipped out his pistol to fire at the stranger. He fired over the man's head; he might be a pilgrim, wandering from one town to the next. The horseman spurred toward the trees, and Wicker fired several more times, punched out the shells, and reloaded, then ran back to his horse. Dan was already mounted.

"What was it?"

"I dunno—some *hombre* came along the trail. Could be a posse behind him."

They loped away. Laskovy said, "You only saw one?"

"Yes."

"You hit 'im?"

"No. He was a long way off anyway. . . ."

Laskovy persisted. "You figger they could get a posse after us that quick?"

"No. Probably some picker down on his luck. He'll sit there till daylight."

Laskovy reined in to a walk. "Gettin' too goddam dark to see. You figger that pilgrim back there knows this trail?"

"How the hell would I know what he knows?"

"Well, he thinks there's only one of us."

Rufe grinned. "Well, that's his headboard, ain't it?"

They walked the horses in silence for a time. They came to a broad valley, and the moon appeared, lopsided and ice-white, providing hardly any light to see by, but the trail seemed to cut across the valley, a slightly darker smear than the surrounding fields.

In the trees on the far side they halted. It was a good place to bed down, and Rufe took the first watch, sitting with his back to a tree, the Winchester across his knees.

Chapter Twenty-three

LAREDO got up and stretched in first light. Far overhead a V of geese was reaching southward, probably getting a late start. The sky was mottled, and the day was cold and portended rain. A few nebulous wraiths of mist curled about the treetops near him.

Where was Pete? Well, Pete could take care of himself, no worries about that. Pete would guess he had close-followed Wicker and Laskovy.

He examined the trail, walking along on the weeds beside it. Horses had passed recently, so Wicker hadn't turned off. He found three stones and put them in the middle of the trail, one atop the other, for Pete to find. Then he went on.

When he came to a broad valley, he halted out of sight of it and crawled forward to look. The trail cut across the valley and disappeared into the trees on the far side. Laredo smiled. He had never seen a better place for an ambush.

Wicker had shot at him earlier, but he was positive Wicker had no idea who he was. Did Wicker think he was being followed? If so, he would be sitting under those far trees, waiting for someone to cross the valley toward him.

Laredo went back to the horse. He had to assume that was exactly what Wicker was doing. He looked carefully at the valley and turned left to go around. In an hour or two, if no one came across the valley, Wicker would have to figure one of two things: no one followed him, or someone was doing exactly what he, Laredo, was about—flanking him.

Wicker had half a dozen options. And he was dangerous as a cornered rattler.

It took several hours to make his way in the shelter of the trees leftward. When he again approached the valley, he was miles from the trail. He found a cleft in the hill and followed it slowly. He guessed it would bring him out a mile or so south of the trees where Wicker might be waiting—or had he gone long ago?

When he came at last to the trail, the horse tracks were fresh. Two horses had passed that way very recently.

Laredo went back to the valley and quickly found the spot where Wicker and Laskovy had waited, watching their backtrail. Laredo smiled grimly. The two owlhoots were probably convinced now no one followed them.

He rode across the valley and left another pile of stones for Pete.

Rufe Wicker was reasonably satisfied, he said, the man he'd seen and fired at was a pilgrim or someone who lived in the vicinity. "There's no posse following us."

No one came across the valley toward them.

After waiting an hour after sunup, Dan Laskovy began to move about restlessly. "Let's go on . . . 'fore we get caught in the rain."

"How you going to keep from gettin' caught in the rain?"

"I was hoping we'd find us a shack or something."

Rufe climbed onto his horse. "Hell, there ain't a shack or a house within a hunnerd miles in any direction."

"There better be a town closer'n that. . . ."

It began to drizzle in the next hour, and they rode with heads bent. The sky darkened, and a chill wind searched them with icy fingers. Rufe said, "Gettin' cold enough to snow. . . ."

"Rather have rain."

"Keep a lookout for that shack you was talking about."

Dan growled deep in his throat. This was the worst part of their trade—keeping on the dodge. He sighed inwardly, thinking of Beatrice in Pueblo. He had been a mite quick in judgment probably—he had known what she was. Well, he hadn't beaten her too badly. She was doubtless up and around by now.

The man was another thing. Dan smiled. The *hombre* would be walking around hell with three holes in him, sucking air.

The drizzle continued as if it could not make up its mind to rain. They came out of the hills into the flats, and it got colder. They could see hazy brown ridges far off to the left, and the trail petered out.

Rufe reined in, looking about. "Don't see your shack. . . ."

"Don't see any damned thing." Dan surveyed the horizons. There was no hint of sun anywhere; the dark sky blended with the plain—it was probably raining hard to the right. They heard the far-off rumble of thunder.

"Storm's lookin' for us." Rufe turned to the left. "Let's hit for them hills. . . . Maybe we can find us a cave."

It took several hours to cross the flats to the hills. A few windswept gusts of rain pattered over them, and the misty day closed in. They rode into a dark tide of pines and halted to look back. They could see nothing but the mist.

The thunder was coming closer, rumbling like giant ninepins knocked askew by some careless hand. Rufe's teeth chattered. "We got to find us a place to build a fire."

They rode around the slope of the first hill and found a rocky creek bed, with water just beginning to trickle and splash among the rocks and spread out over the wet sand. The rain found them there, huge drops slamming into them at first, then settling to a steady downpour.

They followed the creek into a narrow canyon with steep sides, and Dan gave a yell, pointing. In ages past water had undercut the side, forming one long cave a dozen feet above the canyon floor. The horses scrambled up the slope, and they got down onto dry sand.

Finding wood to burn was not easy. There was brush in the long cave, but it would last a very short while. Dan went into the rain and came back with driftwood. Rufe made a fire with flint and a D-shaped piece of steel. The brush burned fast, but it dried the large pieces of driftwood, and in half an hour they had a roaring fire that made the day look a good deal better.

"But where the hell are we?" Dan asked.

Wicker shrugged. "We're probably lost. But if we keep goin' south, we're bound to hit Mexico."

Laskovy grunted.

Laredo followed the trail till it petered out in the flats and the rain began to fall. Before it washed out the tracks, he was able to follow them to the left, toward the distant hills. He left more stones for Pete and pointed that way.

Thunder rumbled overhead, and off to the right lightning flashed again and again, and the rain pounded him, limiting visibility to a few hundred yards.

It was a long, miserable, wet ride to the hills. There were no tracks to follow, but there were trees for shelter. He dismounted and huddled under a clump of pines, staring out at the rain. Wicker and Laskovy could be within fifty feet and be invisible. If he made a fire . . .

He made himself as comfortable as possible under the trees to wait out the storm. The pall passed slowly overhead, the thunder muttering off to the east and the rain slackening and finally becoming a foggy drizzle, then it, too, drifted away as night fell.

He slept fitfully and got up, stiff and tired at dawn. What wouldn't he give for a fire!

He rode south, over the hills and down into the plain again without seeing tracks of any kind. The owlhoots had turned south every time: he had to assume they would once more. But now his hopes were thin. The storm had come between them and might have driven them east or west— he had probably lost them again.

He went directly south, navigating by guess, leaving stones for Pete every few miles. The weather moderated, and toward evening the sun came out for a few brief minutes to prove it was still there.

As it became dark he saw the lights of a town, glimmering golden, in the far distance. He came to a road and followed it into the town, a tiny little burg of a dozen shacks and houses, a stage stop its only reason for existence.

The town was called Hadley, a crossroads stopping place without a telegraph. It had a general store, a large stable with a long corral behind it, a photographer's shop, a tiny dry goods store, a blacksmith shop, and four saloons. Around the single main street, behind the store buildings, was a straggle of houses, shacks, and a few weathered and patched tents.

It looked poor, but not begging, and when he rode in, nothing was open but the stable and the saloons. The stable owner was in a back storeroom playing cards with two others under a green glass lantern. Yes, Laredo could bed down in a stall. "Two bits, mister. Feed your horse for two bits more."

It was a Tuesday night. A few cowboys were in town, the owner said, but they would probably be gone back to their outfits before another hour passed. Then the town would go to sleep. He looked at the photo of Wicker and shook his head. "Ain't seem 'im."

There was no place in town to get a bath. But there was a creek with a good-sized water hole about a mile out of town. Most went there with soap and towel when they felt the urge, the man told him. "Course it's wintertime now— water's probably colder'n a polar bear's ass. You want a bath, you better do'er out'n a basin."

He was a potato-shaped man with a bowler hat and yellow suspenders over a dark blue shirt. He went back to his card game, and Laredo bedded down for the night.

The morning dawned crisp and clear, the storm long gone but leaving deep furrows in the street, with occasional puddles. Laredo had breakfast in the nearby saloon and talked with the bartender, a skinny, sad-eyed man who had not seen Wicker either. The bartender studied the sheet and

142

handed it back. Had Laredo heard anything of a railroad spur coming their way from the north?

He had not, Laredo said, and the man went away seemingly sadder than ever.

There was no law in the town. The nearest deputy was at Ridgefield, they told him, forty-some miles to the west. There had been talk of hiring a town marshal, but nothing had been done. The largest saloon had a bouncer who kept order.... There were no women in the town at all; there had been one, but she had died several years past. Occasionally, the blacksmith said, a woman came through the town on a wagon—going somewhere else with her husband—and a crowd of men would turn out to stare at her as the wagon went by. If it stopped they would gather around....

It was evening when Laredo, in the stable, saw two riders go by in the street. Was one of them Wicker? He hurried to the door in time to see them step down in front of a saloon near the edge of town. The taller looked very much like Wicker.

There were half a dozen horses at the hitchracks by the saloon. Probably the place was very busy this time of night. If he entered the saloon, would Wicker recognize him as the man he'd shot at several days ago? If he did, would he pull a pistol and start shooting again? Crowded saloon or not? It was very possible.

If he did, Laredo would have to shoot back, and in the crowd it was likely some bystander would die. Laskovy would be shooting, too—he was known to be as quick with a gun as Wicker. It would be a madhouse with all the gunsmoke and shouting....

It would be best to wait for the two to come out. With a little luck he would get the drop on them.

He walked to the saloon and positioned himself directly across the street from the bat-wing doors. He felt a certain nervousness. He was about to face two very experienced gunmen—they could come out any moment. He had not felt so alone in a long time, with only Colonel Colt to keep him company. He should have waited for Pete a day or two ago.

He half sat against a hitchrack and watched men come and go from the saloon. A few piled on horses and rode off. Others hung about, talking and spitting, drifting on down the street, still talking.

Laredo looked at the sky. It was not as cold as it had been, though still overcast. He flexed his fingers and rubbed his hands together, keeping them warm.

An hour passed before Dan Laskovy came out of the saloon. He went to his horse and pulled at the cinch straps.

Laredo waited for Wicker, but he did not appear.

As Laskovy was about to mount Laredo walked into the street toward him.

Chapter Twenty-four

RUFE was tired of running, he said. He was sure a posse was on their trail, and Dan could not talk him out of the idea. Of course it was foolishness to try to outfight a posse, so there was nothing to do but outdistance them or confuse them somehow. . . .

While they argued they came to Hadley, a settlement poor and run-down as any plank and batten collection of shacks they had ever seen.

The town had no telegraph, which pleased Rufe; it meant they got their news a week or more late . . . if they got it then.

They stepped down in front of the saloon as it was getting dark. The place was a deadfall, but it had a wood floor and a kitchen of sorts. A few men eyed them as they entered, but no one stared as they took a table in the back.

The food served them was terrible and the coffee bitter, but it was pleasant being inside for a change, listening to voices instead of the wind. The town had no hotel, but they might be able to put up at the stable, the barman said. So after a bit Dan got up to go make the arrangements.

When he went outside, it was dark and there was no one around, except a man on the far side of the rutted street. Laskovy fiddled with the cinch straps of the horse as he eyed the stranger beneath the brim of his hat. The man seemed interested in him. Was he a bounty hunter?

As the man stepped into the street Dan slid the Colt from his belt and cocked it. If it came to shooting, Rufe would be out the door in a moment, backing him up.

He heard the stranger say "Put your hands on the saddle where I can see 'em."

Instead Dan turned and fired.

He saw the flash and smoke as the other pistol fired at the same time.

Laredo swore under his breath as he saw Laskovy crumple, the pistol falling from his nerveless hand. He hadn't wanted to kill the man. But when he reached the downed man, there was no doubt of it: Laskovy had been centered.

Men erupted from the saloon, but Rufe was not among them. Someone brought a lantern, and they turned the body over. Someone remarked, "The hole's in the front. . . ."

They looked at Laredo, who said, "He fired at me. Did he have a friend inside?"

He did, but no one knew what had happened to him.

Laredo went into the saloon, which was empty. The Mexican in the kitchen told him a man had come through it in a hurry. Laredo described Wicker, and the man nodded.

It was dark behind the saloon. There was a broken-down wagon and heaps of trash, then the prairie. He prowled along behind the buildings but saw no one.

When he went back to the street, some men were putting the body into a buckboard. They would haul it to the next town for burial. There was no preacher or undertaker in Hadley. A man had a right to both, even if he was an owlhoot. His last journey ought to be made properly.

Laredo bought drinks all round, then went back to the livery stable. Wicker had gotten away again. Doubtless when he'd heard the shooting, he had made himself scarce.

In the morning Laredo heard a horse had been stolen the night before. It had been tied at the far end of town. So Wicker had hotfooted it behind the buildings, as Laredo suspected, stolen the horse, and disappeared. He might have nearly brushed by Wicker as he searched for the man.

So the animal tied in front of the saloon was Wicker's.

There was nothing but the saddle and a rifle left behind. If Wicker still had loot, he had it with him.

The man who had lost the horse took Wicker's; it was only fair.

Laredo wrote out an account of the shooting and gave it to the man who was to drive the wagon. The man would give it to the first lawman he encountered.

Dan Laskovy had had considerable money on his person—more than five thousand dollars, in fact. But there were no letters or other identification. Laredo showed his credentials to the interested men, and it was agreed by them that he would turn the money over to the law himself when he explained it was undoubtedly U.S. army money, part of the payroll robbery.

Where had Wicker gone?

Would he continue south, or would he consider himself closely pursued, now that his partner was violently dead? If so, he might run any direction.

Or he might go south, figuring his pursuers would think that his last choice now. How could you second-guess an outlaw?

He might go to join the Porter brothers again.

A lot of questions.

He was sitting in the saloon with a beer before him, considering his options, when a man came in asking for him. "You the feller shot the outlaw gent last night?"

"I'm afraid so. . . ." Laredo admitted.

The man sat opposite him at the table. "It was my horse his friend stole. Reckon I ought to tell you—that horse was not much. I figger he wouldn't last ten mile. It musta been dark when he stole that nag. That feller is afoot by now."

He was.

Rufe had had no time to inspect horseflesh. The animal had a saddle and bridle; it was the nearest horse tied to the hitchrack; he mounted and turned away from town into the dark.

Immediately, however, he realized the horse was stumbling, shambling along like a half-dead mule. He swore aloud, but he dared not go back. The horse was willing to travel at a walk, but when spurred into a lope, Wicker feared it would collapse.

He headed north, backtracking toward the hills.

Had someone fired at Dan? He had moved at the first sounds of shooting—there had been only two shots—had run out through the kitchen and turned right along the backs of the few stores. Dan was on his own. If he had run into a bounty hunter, that was his luck, good or bad.

The horse lasted maybe five miles before halting, head down, unable to go any farther. Rufe was disgusted. He would have shot the animal but for the noise.

He pulled off the saddlebags and went on, swearing at his luck. He was in a very dangerous position—on the formless prairie with nowhere to hide. If someone suspected he might have gone north, and looked for him, he could be taken easily. A man afoot was almost helpless.

He had no rifle. His rifle had been left with the horse in front of the saloon. He had thousands of dollars in the saddlebags, but now the money was only dead weight. He couldn't buy a horse. . . .

He walked all day, with long pauses for rest; he was unused to walking, especially with the fancy boots he wore, and his feet and calves ached in a few hours.

By late afternoon he was sure he could see the distant hills in the haze. It was clouding up again and turning cold. He had left his blanket roll on the horse, too. . . . It was going to be a hard night.

Pete Torres halted as he came out of the low hills. Before him was the vast plain, rolling away toward Mexico. He looked at the sky; the sun had gone, and it would be dark very shortly. There was a creek a few yards to his right, and a stand of pines.

In front of him was a tiny pile of stones. Laredo had come this way. He must be close behind Wicker and Laskovy.

Pete kicked the stones apart and made camp in the trees by the creek. He dug a deep hole and made a tiny fire to make coffee and heat strips of dried meat.

Then he rolled a cigarette and wondered what Laredo was about. As he lit the cigarette a voice said, "Stand up and put your hands out."

Pete dropped the cigarette and jumped up in astonishment. *"Caramba!"* He did as he was told, and his first quick glance at the intruder told him it was Wicker himself! And Wicker held a six-gun on him.

The man looked tired and dirty and had worn saddlebags over his left shoulder. How had he crept up so silently?

Pete instantly adopted a stumbling English: "W'at ees eet, *señor*?"

"I need your horse."

"But, but—*señor*!"

"You want to argue?" Wicker pulled the hammer back on the Colt.

Pete shook his head, shrugging. "No, *señor....*" This man was a killer. He stared at the unwavering muzzle of the .45.

Wicker untied the horse, mounted, and looked down at him. "Toss your gun over there in the weeds."

Pete did as he was told, hoping he looked to Wicker as a simple Mexican, eager to cause no trouble. He saw the man smile; Wicker was obviously satisfied. He nudged the horse and rode off quickly. Pete scrambled for his pistol, but Wicker had disappeared in the gloom.

What the hell had happened to Wicker's horse?

Pete sighed and sat down dejectedly. He had made only a tiny fire, but apparently it had been seen—or a reflection of it. He was surprised Wicker had been able to creep up so close without being detected. Pete swore at himself; he had probably been half-asleep.

He got out the makin's. Had Wicker and Laredo met? Had something happened to Laredo? Why was Wicker afoot?

And why was he alone?

Questions with no answers.

He lit the brown cigarette and puffed thoughtfully. Now he had a decision to make: should he stay here, or should he follow the stones Laredo had set out? He had no idea where the trail led—he might have to walk for a week to get to a town.

He had the horseman's dislike of walking, but maybe Laredo was lying out there on the prairie, needing help.

That decided him. He set out at first light, the blanket roll over one shoulder. It was cold yet clear, though clouds were building up in the west, and the air began to smell like rain again.

There was no trail; it had petered out when he hit the plain. But in a mile or so was another small cairn of stones. He was on the right track.

When he came to the top of a higher swale, he paused and surveyed the land as far as he could see in every direction, but nothing moved but the distant clouds and a few hawks circling and sliding down silently to pounce on lunch in the sea of grass.

Just after midday he saw a horseman . . . coming toward him. Pete lay flat, his six-gun extended. Wicker had taken his rifle with the horse.

The rider was Laredo, and he had been seen.

Pete got up, and Laredo galloped toward him and jumped down. "What happened to you?"

"Wicker. He needed a horse."

"Yes. He stole one in town, a poor nag. I passed it a while back. It put him afoot. How did he get yours?"

Pete explained, in disgusted tones. "I pulled my forelock for him, so I suppose he didn't think I was worth shooting. Why wasn't Laskovy with him?"

Laredo filled him in on the happenings in Hadley. "So you figure he's headed north again?"

"That's the way he went." Pete shrugged.

"I thought you were gonna show him your diploma."

Pete sighed deeply. "I forgot."

They went back to the hills, riding double, and looked for Wicker's trail. It was not difficult to follow in the soft earth. The outlaw was definitely heading north.

Pete said, "Maybe it was Laskovy who wanted to go south."

"Well, he certainly changed his mind. . . ."

Chapter Twenty-five

Rufe laughed to himself as he rode away. The poor dumb Mexican had been in exactly the right place at the right time. He ought to go back and thank him. It was a good horse, a worn but very good saddle, and a fine Winchester in the boot.

From feeling tired and miserable an hour ago, he now was elated.

If the shots back in the town meant a bounty hunter was after them—and had fired at Dan—then maybe someone was tracking them. That someone would know they had been heading south for days. If he now reversed himself and went due north, it might throw him or them off completely.

Except for that damned miserable crowbait he had ridden out of town. Well, he would have to chance that. Now it might be smart to go hook up with the Porters again.

What *had* happened to Dan? Probably he had been shot at and had skedaddled; possibly he'd been forced to run south. Well, whatever, they would get back together again one day. He'd leave a message for Dan with Henry Whitaker.

There was no telling where the Porter brothers were. Maybe at Lyden, only that was a far piece. But they probably hung out somewhere along the tracks. They were fond of railroads.

He avoided the trail they had used to come south and bent far eastward. He was probably in Indian territory, though he had seen no redskins. It worried him slightly, because a white man traveling alone was fair game for the wild tribes. They would chase him down, if only for his rifle.

He decided to lay up during the day and travel by night. He would make less time, but he was in no big hurry, and he might save his hair. A pilgrim on a horse could be seen for miles, and a trap laid for him.

He found a convenient overhang and got down wearily to make a tiny fire before dark. He boiled coffee and ate tough meat, then rested for several hours.

When he started out again, he could not consult the stars because of the overcast, but at least it was not raining. He started north, depending on his instincts to guide him in a reasonably straight line. A cold wind accompanied him, moaning now and then like a disappointed ghost, and toward morning a drizzle set upon him, icy and feathery, pinching his cheeks.

He halted at dawn, looking for a likely spot and found it in a jumble of rocks that had slid down a mountain ages ago.

Safe in a cleft of rocks, he made a small fire for coffee and comfort, broiled all the meat he had, and smoked a cheroot. Why not go north to Lyden? It was a big town to get lost in. He could change his name and appearance, and no one would be the wiser. In a small town people were nosy, wanting to know everything they could because they had nothing better to do. Also, from Lyden he could put out word for the Porters.

Dan would probably guess that's where he had gone, and sooner or later would join up.

The decision made, Wicker put out the fire and curled up to sleep.

The nearest telegraph was north, and since Wicker had last been seen heading north, they went that way, following Wicker's tracks.

The weather held, cold but not raining, and they made slow time riding double. They lost the trail several times, found it again, and pressed on. But when they came to a wide rocky area where nothing grew, they lost it, and darkness fell before they picked it up again.

It rained moderately for an hour or so during the night, and in the morning they could find no tracks at all.

Laredo sighed deeply. "We may as well get to a telegraph. What's your vote?"

"I vote for a horse."

The weather turned fickle, drizzling then sun for a short spell till the clouds closed over again. The clouds won out, and it rained for an hour as they waited under trees.

In late afternoon they came to a well-defined road, with parallel tracks growing weeds down the center, which meant wheeled traffic. They followed the road as it swerved off to the east, then north again to edge a region of deep ravines, and at nightfall came to Benton, a town built around a stageline and a freighting yard.

The freighting company, Madison, Howard, and Ayres, employed about half the town, they were told. The company owned the only hotel and several of the saloons.

The town law, George Bannick, knew who Rufe Wicker was but had not seen him in person ever. "He ain't come through here. Wish he would, though. Like to git my hands on that reward."

The livery had half a dozen horses for sale, and Pete picked out a good-looking sorrel and a saddle while Laredo wired John Fleming to report. They had accomplished half the mission with Dan Laskovy's death. But Wicker's whereabouts were unknown.

Fleming's wire said the Porters were west of St. Louis and might be at Lyden again. They had taken a stagecoach from somewhere in Kansas, and their tail had lost them. He suggested perhaps they were in communication with Wicker and might join up with him.

Laredo agreed and wired that he and Pete would go to Lyden to see what they could scare up.

They stayed overnight at the hotel, had baths, and rode

153

out in the morning, pointing toward Lyden, bucking a heavy wind. In the forenoon they came across a wagon train with mules and oxen plodding along, hauling canvas-topped prairie wagons loaded with white bones and furniture, including a piano.

They halted to exchange news. The wagons had had a brush with Comanche, the wagon master told them. The Indians had appeared out of nowhere and made several passes at them, killing one mule.

"We scared 'em off with rifles—they shook their fists at us and went off thataway." He pointed south.

"We haven't seen any," Laredo said.

"Well, it's late for 'em. They probably sittin' around somewheres eatin' the grub the gover'ment hands out. The goddam gover'ment ever do anything right?"

"Not that I know of," Laredo said solemnly.

The wagon master sighed and looked at the sky. "Goin' to rain, the way the flies take holt."

When they came at last to the rails, they turned west and followed them to Lyden.

The day they arrived it began to snow.

An hour devoted to talking to hotel clerks turned up nothing. No one had seen a man resembling Wicker.

"He's probably in Texas," Pete said, "a thousand miles from here."

Wicker rode into the town of Alamar, freezing cold. He put the horse in the hotel stable and had the stableboy build a fire under a tank of water.

"Pour it into a tub so's I c'n take a bath. Then you run out and buy me a paper." He gave the boy a dime.

The hot water thawed him out. He soaked, smoking a cheroot, and felt better than he had in days. A hot bath when it was cold as hell outside was a real luxury.

When the boy brought the newspaper, he turned the pages idly. The national news did not interest him, but on a back page he saw the item: WELL-KNOWN OUTLAW KILLED IN HADLEY.

Wicker sat up abruptly. Dan Laskovy was dead!

He read the item several times; it was brief. Laskovy had been killed in a gunfight with a federal officer who was not named. Laskovy had refused to surrender outside a saloon, had drawn his pistol instead, and had lost. He had been buried in the town's Boot Hill.

Wicker dropped the paper. Jesus! Dan was dead! He put his head back and closed his eyes. Goddam!

He picked up the paper and read the item again. What had happened to the money Dan had been packing? The paper said nothing about it. Wicker sighed. Probably some local sheriff's deputy had pocketed it and kept his mouth shut.

A federal officer had shot Dan? Why were the federals in the case—because they had robbed the army payroll? Probably. Wicker stared at the opposite wall. Was that federal officer now after *him*? It was very damned likely.

He got out of the tub, toweled and dressed, slung the saddlebags over his shoulder, and went down the street to a restaurant.

The best thing for him to do was go to Lyden and get a message to the Porter brothers. They had agreed on names for messages to be left with hotel clerks. He wondered if they were being tracked by federals, too. He ate a steak and drank coffee and went back to the hotel. No one had followed him here. There had been no one within miles when he had taken the Mexican's horse. He had no bill of sale for the animal, but probably not one rider out of a thousand had such a document.

No, he was safe enough—so long as no one recognized him. He had not seen one of the damned posters with his face on it for quite a while. That was reassuring.

He went to sleep early and got up as a rooster began to crow in back of the hotel. He dressed and went downstairs to the street. The restaurant was open, and he had breakfast, and asked them about the stagecoach. It went as far as Lyden, they told him. After he ate, he walked to the waiting room and looked at the schedule. The stage went to Lyden, all right, and he could get it that afternoon. He

155

went to the front window and stared out at the street. The weather was turning colder. Wouldn't it be warmer riding in the coach than on horseback for days?

He went to the livery and made a deal for the horse and saddle, telling the man he was going to the railroad to take the train west.

He kept the Winchester rifle and boarded the stage that afternoon with several other passengers. The weather was crisp and cold, and they rode for more than three hours to reach a tiny settlement calling itself Boyd's. There were cubicles for the passengers, a bar and restaurant, several corrals, and a fenced area with sheds for the coach.

As customary, they had introduced themselves when they got settled in the coach. Wicker called himself Winters. He sat opposite a thin-faced middle-aged man who said his name was Evans and that he was a book-keeper by trade. Wicker thought him very shifty-eyed. Evans seemed to stare at him a great deal, never meeting Wicker's eyes.

He got away from the man when they got to Boyd's. He was assigned room 4 and went into it at once, to stay there until the bell rang to signal supper was on the table.

Wicker ate quickly, avoiding Evans, and went back to his room—had the man recognized him, or thought he had?

It was drizzling when they got up the next morning, but as they finished breakfast the drizzle stopped and they went on. Every creek they crossed was running full, but no bridges were out. One of the passengers assured them all he traveled this road frequently and a great deal of work had been done on the road and bridges only last year.

At about midday they came to another station like Boyd's. Coach horses were changed, and the passengers got a hot meal. Wicker was conscious that Evans seemed to be studying him from the next table. Had he better do something about the man? Maybe Evans was waiting till a lawman showed up.

He followed the slim man outside. The building had a large overhang, shelter from a summer sun. Evans was not in front of the place. Wicker peered along the side of the

156

building. Evans was several rods away, looking at a paper he had taken from his pocket. It was one of the wanted sheets with Wicker's picture on it.

Wicker took a long breath. He could shoot the sonofabitch now—but what excuse would he give? It was always a good idea to have a solid reason for ventilating another citizen. It would certainly make everyone look very carefully at him. He wondered if Evans was armed. If so, he might provoke the man into drawing his weapon.

Or should he wait for nightfall . . . and go to Evans's room, rap on the door, and finish him then?

Wicker smiled.

He went back into the room and had a drink at the short bar in the corner, lighting a cigar.

Lyden was not far away, the driver told him. If the weather held and there was no trouble along the road, they would reach Lyden in another day.

He would have to do it tonight.

Chapter Twenty-six

THERE was nothing to do, as Laredo said, but plod from one place to another and ask questions, show the photo of Wicker, and hope for the best.

Every madam on the line shook her head at them. None had seen the man—if they could be believed. Pete did not believe them.

"We're trying to pull in one of their customers. Are they going to tell us the truth?" Torres asked.

"Guess not," Laredo admitted.

There was somewhat the same problem with bartenders. A few seemed open about looking at the photo, but most were monumentally uninterested. They served anyone who came in and stood at the bar. If Satan himself had two bits, he could get a drink.

Hotel clerks were the easiest to talk to, but none had seen Wicker. The town was a dead end ... maybe. There were plenty of places Wicker could be staying, private homes or shacked up with some girl. . . . They might search all year and not find him.

The first snow did not stay on the ground. But it turned very cold for days. Laredo and Pete put up at the Stanton Hotel and talked with Vernon Stokes, the local marshal, every day or two.

Stokes said he'd had many conversations with Phil Bowers before they had hanged him. Wicker was the wily one, Bowers had told him. You couldn't trust Wicker at all. The Porter brothers were more outgoing and easy to deal with, except they wanted things their own way. Somehow they got along with Wicker. They were both pretty tough, and maybe Wicker hadn't wanted to tangle with them.

Bowers had no idea where Wicker might hole up or go. His best advice was "Don't let Wicker get behind you."

Wicker waited for nightfall. He spent the evening in the little bar that was part of the restaurant. But he drank sparingly, and when the lights were turned out, he went back to his cubicle for an hour or so. The door had no lock, only a short piece of slat that pivoted on a nail to keep the door closed. Any push would force the door open. And each of the cubicles were the same. The owner had spent no money on security.

It was very dark when he went outside again. He had to almost feel his way to the kitchen. That door had the same kind of lock, and he pushed in easily, scratched a match, and picked a long knife off a serving table.

He didn't want to use his own knife; it would be too easy to miss bloodstains in the dark.

Making certain he was not observed, he went at once to Evans's room, peered around for a moment, looking for movement, then pushed the door open. It made a squeaking noise, and the sleeper stirred. Wicker closed the door behind him, scratched a match, and lit the stub of candle on the box by the cot. He bent and held Evans's head tightly and shoved the blade in behind the ear. The victim jerked and coughed—then nothing.

Wicker waited a moment to make sure the job was done. Evans had no pulse. He felt nothing for the man; Evans had brought it on himself, the fool.

He went through his victim's clothes, found the wanted sheet, and crumpled it into his pocket. He left the knife where it was, blew out the candle, and let himself out. A coyote howled a long way off as he went to his own room.

159

In the morning shouts woke him, and he dressed quickly and stepped outside. "What's the matter?"

One of the passengers said, "Evans got dead last night."

Wicker was as astonished as everyone else. Who had done it—and why? Another of the passengers said at breakfast, "Nobody knew him well enough to kill him."

It was a mystery. The body hadn't been robbed. The station owner was in a dither, not knowing what to do. Such a thing had never happened before. There had been deaths, but no outright murders.

It was something for the police to handle, but the stage-coach driver refused to take the body to the next town, arguing he had no place to put it. The luggage boot was full, and he would not have it on top, and the passengers would not have it inside. The law would have to come to the station.

The owner finally decided he would bury the body, and the driver agreed to mention the killing to the law. So after breakfast they got moving again.

It began to snow lightly as the coach moved onto the road, and the passengers unrolled blankets and wrapped themselves in. The coach had no glass, only flimsy screens on the windows, and the wind howled through. But the snow did not stick, and after an hour it turned to drizzle.

It took forever to get to Lyden.

The Porter brothers were in the same hotel, the Travelers' Home Inn, near the railroad station, registered as Frederick and Thomas Shultz, the names they had agreed upon with Wicker.

Their meeting was more somber because of the deaths of Phil Bowers and Dan Laskovy but, as Gus Porter said, "You take your chances, and some get caught."

The brothers had been in town only a few days and had nothing lined up. Quinn told Wicker, "Our man at the fort says the payroll is coming a different way now, and it's more secret."

"The army finally learned," Gus said. "They must have some new blood running things."

"There's always banks," Wicker observed.

"We never went into the bank business," Quinn said, looking at his brother. "How d'you know what's in a bank vault?"

"There's guesswork," Wicker admitted. "But there's always something—banks deal in money, after all."

"This's winter," Gus said. "How much business does a bank do in winter?"

Wicker lit a cheroot. "Banks make money loaning out money, and they get payments all year long. I'd figger they got to have *some* money on hand."

"Well, there's gettin' away," Quinn said, "in wintertime."

"You got to get away when you rob a train, too . . ." —Wicker blew smoke—"and if we got a minute to plan it right, there's a way to beat a posse."

Gus looked interested. "Go on . . ."

"Well, you look a bank over and decide to take it. Then you decide which day to do 'er. So you stake out some horses five, six miles from town. Nice fresh horses. When you run out'n the bank, you head for them horses with the posse after you. You ride like hell, then switch horses, and the posse never catches up."

Quinn laughed, and Gus said, "Pretty slick." He went to the window. "But like I said, it's wintertime. They'll track you in the snow."

Wicker nodded. "You got to pick the right day. It don't snow all the time. And even in the snow, if it snows hard enough, it'll cover tracks in a jiffy."

"You've done this before?" Quinn asked.

Wicker nodded again. "More'n once."

There were two banks in Lyden, and both seemed well-guarded. Wicker and the two Porters looked them over at different times. When they met again in the inn to discuss the matter, Wicker thought the banks too well guarded.

"I don't like the odds."

"They's three of us," Gus said. "We go in shootin', and the guards is gone in a second."

"And ever'body in town knows it—I mean, you go in shootin' and they'll hear it in St. Louie." Wicker shook his

161

head. "You got to give 'em credit," Wicker said stubbornly. "You plan for things and if they don't happen, well, that's fine. But you can't plan when you're on a horse ridin' out fast."

"He's got a point," Quinn said.

Gus frowned. "You don't like either of the banks here? Then what you got in mind? If we hit one of them small banks out in the country, there won't be much in the safe."

Wicker made a face. "You hit three or four of them and there is. Me and Dan got eighteen thousand out of one small bank. Took us five minutes and no posse."

Gus stared at him. "And you killed three people if I r'member."

"How many did you kill at Willows?"

Quinn said, "Wait a minute. Don't let's get to quarrelin'. Have a drink, Rufe."

Gus fished for a cigar. "We got to think on this some more. We hit three or four banks that increases the odds, don't it? We'll have three or four posses after us."

"Not if we plan it smart. They can't catch us if they can't find us."

"You got something in mind?" Quinn asked.

Wicker sat opposite Gus. "If we hit a bank near a railroad station, for instance, maybe twenty miles away. We know when the train is due. We hit the bank, ride to the depot, and get on the train. The next day we're a hunnerd miles down the road.

Gus smiled. "Well, now, that listens better. We pay the railroad to make our getaway."

Rufe stayed indoors during the day, but when he got restless, he went down to the saloon close to the depot. With his hat tipped over his eyes he sat by the wall with a beer before him and listened to the chatter and watched the girls.

He did not notice Adele, the girl he had taken up with the last time he'd been in town. She walked close by him as she talked with another customer, and got a good look at him. He had changed very little.

162

She had bleached her hair and looked very different. His eyes passed over her without recognition. She was startled and instantly thought of the reward. She had read it was up to twelve hundred dollars!

The next day she went to see Marshal Vernon Stokes. "Rufe Wicker is back in town!"

"Wicker!" He was surprised.

"I saw him at the Red Horse last night."

"You sure?"

She blew out her breath. "Of course I'm sure! He sat there for more than an hour . . . alone."

"Did you talk to him?"

"No, course not. He didn't recognize me. He didn't talk to no one that I saw. The paper says he's worth twelve hundred, Marshal. This time I want it!"

"You didn't see where he went?"

"No."

"All right. You go on. Lemme handle this. . . ." He shooed her out. Stokes had three deputies. He called them in, showed them pictures of Wicker, and told them what Adele had said.

"Don't none of you try to take this man alone. You-all ask at every hotel near the saloon. Maybe he's livin' close by. Meet me at the depot in two hours."

At the depot Stokes looked at schedules. No train had stopped at the station last night. Probably the fact that the saloon was near the railroad station was coincidence.

When his deputies arrived, one had struck pay dirt. "He's staying at the Travelers' Home down the street. Registered as Ben Hammond."

"Is he in?"

"The clerk says he is."

They rode to the hotel, and Stokes looked it over critically, walking through the stable and peering at the outside of the hotel.

The clerk showed him Wicker's room. It was off a narrow hallway on the first floor. He went outside again and looked at Wicker's two windows from a short distance where he would not be noticed. The windows faced clumps of shrubbery, but an agile man could easily jump out without trouble.

Stokes decided he would need more men if he tried to pry Wicker out of the room.

"When does he come out?" he asked the clerk.

The man shrugged. "To eat." He pointed to a wall clock. "He ought to come out for lunch."

"Does he go to the hotel restaurant?"

"No. He usually eats in his room."

Stokes blew out his breath. "You just told me he ought to come out for lunch."

"Well, he got to come here to the desk to order it. Then we deliver it to his room."

"I see." Stokes considered. That's where he would take the outlaw. He told his men, "I'll be behind the desk, looking like a bookkeeper. When he comes to the desk, you three come up behind him. No shooting unless there's no other way. You hear me?"

It went like clockwork. Stokes sat behind the desk with the nervous clerk. He put on a pair of glasses, took off his coat, and did his best to look like a bookkeeper, with his pistol on the desk before him covered by a newspaper.

When Wicker came to the desk, he looked sharply at Stokes—then his hands went up as three revolver muzzles poked into his back.

He was quickly disarmed and manacled, and they took him away to the jail. Stokes was astonished at how well it had gone.

Wicker was no less surprised.

Chapter Twenty-seven

LAREDO and Pete heard about Wicker's arrest immediately and went to the jail to talk to Marshal Stokes. Stokes explained about the saloon girl, Adele, and how they had taken Wicker at the hotel.

"With four guns on him he didn't argue."

Laredo asked, "When will the trial take place?"

"That's up to the judge, but I 'spect it will be a month or so. Them lawyers got to shuffle their papers, you know."

"Can we have a look at the jail?" Pete asked.

Stokes showed them the layout. It was an ordinary jail with six cells. Wicker was in the end one, lying on a bunk, staring at them. If he recognized them, he said nothing.

The building was stone with a log roof and looked stout. The marshal's office was in front, with a thick metal door between it and the jail. There was only one door to the outside. No one had ever attempted an escape, the marshal told them. One of his deputies was on duty round the clock. After hours he slept in the office.

Laredo wired John Fleming that Wicker was in the Lyden jail and that they would remain till the trial, unless he had other instructions.

He did. He was wiring the U.S. Marshal for the district to take custody of Wicker, to hold him for trial in a U.S. district court.

Apparently Fleming had little regard for the local justice

system, though it had operated efficiently enough in the case of Phil Bowers. Wicker was a more dangerous killer.

Their instructions were to remain in Lyden until the U.S. Marshal arrived, to confer with him and give whatever depositions were necessary, then to return to Washington.

Their job was over.

Gus and Quinn Porter were outraged that Rufe had been taken by the law. How could it have happened?

"Probably one of them damned wanted sheets," Quinn said. "Somebody turned him in."

Gus agreed. "Never let nobody ever take your picture!"

Quinn knew the offending photograph had been taken in prison and Rufe had had no choice, but he did not mention that to Gus in his present mood.

He said, "Can we get him out?"

"I seen that jail up close," Gus said, nodding. "What we need is a badge."

"A badge?"

"That's right. A lawman's badge." Gus frowned in thought. "We could make a star outa tin; at night it could pass for the real thing." He explained his plan, and Quinn went out to buy a pair of tin snips.

The Lyden jail was on a side street, near the end of the street. The nearest building was forty feet away; the jail was surrounded by vacant lots and a few shacks, with a corral and a small stable on the west side.

At one o'clock in the morning Gus and Quinn saddled their horses, and Rufe's horse, which was still in the hotel stable. At a walk they road to the jailhouse with the third horse. As they got down in front of the squat building, Gus fastened the tin star he and Quinn had made to his lapel.

Then, with Quinn's hands held behind him, as if cuffed, Gus rapped on the door of the jail.

In five minutes the deputy's voice yelled, "What you want?"

"Got a prisoner for the jail," Gus said. "Got to put him in for the night."

"Who're you?"

"Deputy Porter from Comanche County."

The jail door opened, and the sleepy deputy peered at them. He had lit a lantern and held it up to look at them. Gus slammed his revolver barrel across the man's forehead, and the deputy collapsed, dropping the lantern. Oil spattered over the floor, and flames licked up one wall. Quinn swore and dashed the contents of a washbasin on them but the water only scattered the fire.

Gus ran into the back with the jail keys and unlocked the door, yelling at Rufe to get his ass up.

Rufe was awake in a moment. "Izzat you, Gus!?" He swung out of the cot and grabbed his boots. "Is the goddam jail on fire?"

"Get your clothes and hurry up—you can dress later!"

A man in the next cell began to yell, and Gus tossed him the keys as he and Rufe ran out. Smoke was seeping out of the office. Rufe was wearing only long underwear and boots. He grabbed his gun belt and pistol from a peg behind a desk and followed the brothers out to the horses.

The jail walls were afire, flames licking at the log roof. Smoke began to pour out the door. The deputy who had been hit got to his hands and knees as the three mounted and pounded along the street toward the prairie.

He stumbled into the open and fired five shots into the air . . . then sat down in the street, holding his head.

The deputy's shots brought Marshal Stokes to the jail, and he sent for Laredo and Pete Torres.

The fire was out when they arrived, but the jail office was a ruin. The inside had been paneled, and the wood was mostly burned away along with part of a desk. Rufe Wicker was gone, and so was a drunk who had been sleeping it off.

"We leave one man in the jail office when we got prisoners," Stokes explained. "Me and the others takes shifts moseying around the town, and we all got keys to the door. Somebody knew our routine."

He had questioned the hurt deputy, who was home in

bed. "Jerry says a man come to the jail sayin' he was a deputy with a prisoner. He had a badge, too. When he opened the door, the feller hit him." Stokes shook his head, surveying the ruined office. "The council is gonna beat on my ass about this. . . ."

"Only two men?" Laredo asked.

"That's right. And they had a third horse with 'em."

Pete said, "They have an hour's start, *amigo*."

It must have been the Porter brothers, they decided. The hurt deputy had not been able to describe the men very well. It had been dark, and he'd been hit as soon as he raised the lantern.

But Rufe had been a loner, except with Dan Laskovy and the Porters. And Laskovy was gone.

They had headed into the trackless prairie—probably because they knew the fire would attract attention, and they had to make tracks as fast as possible. Where would they go?

"To the nearest railroad," Pete said. "The Porters like railroads."

"There's a railroad in Lyden."

"Maybe they're going to the next depot."

"Which way?" Laredo asked. "East or west? But why would they get on a train? Why wouldn't they hole up? They did it before. Remember Peevy?"

"That's right. Would they go back there?"

Laredo shrugged. "Maybe. They don't know *we* were there."

They waited for dawn, not far off, and looked for tracks . . . and lucked out. The earth was damp from snow and rains, and horse prints were plain on bare ground, heading south. Three horses.

They followed them all that day but did not come in sight of them. Following was slower than running. They lost the tracks several times and had to hunt for them. In the afternoon it began to drizzle.

When night came, they continued southward, walking the horses. They were miles behind the pursued and hoped

168

for sight of a campfire. The three had not varied their direction all day. But they saw no fire. The drizzle stopped, and it was colder.

Near morning they came to a settlement and halted, looking it over. It was a collection of dark shacks and corrals beside a swollen stream. They stepped down beside the rushing water under clumps of cottonwoods and willows to wait for sunup.

At first light they separated. Laredo walked into the settlement from one direction, Pete from the opposite. If the three men had stopped here, it should be obvious. There was no place to hide.

Laredo sidled in, moving slowly. He saw no one. The shacks were built in no particular design, seemingly set down haphazardly. There was no street. He moved past a corral where half a dozen black mules sniffled and stared at him. Beside the corral was a wagon that looked to have been there a very long time.

In front of a large shack with the word STABLE painted on it three horses were tied to the hitchrack.

As Laredo looked, Rufe Wicker came out of the stable and shoved a Winchester into the boot of the end horse. He went back into the stable.

Pete Torres appeared just beyond the shacky building, and Laredo motioned to him, pointing to the stable. Pete nodded. Laredo took a long breath. There was going to be no easy way to do this. All three of these men were desperate characters who would fight to the death rather than surrender to the law.

He flipped open the loading gate of the Colt and inspected the brass. Two men came from the stable. One was Wicker, the other—from the description—was Gus Porter. They were both carrying small cloth sacks, which they tied on behind the cantles. In another few minutes they would be riding out.

Where the hell was Pete? Maybe he had entered the stable from the far end. Wicker and the other were talking as Porter fiddled with cinching up the saddle. Then Porter untied the reins and swung up.

Laredo waited no longer. Pistol in hand, he stepped into the street.

They both saw him instantly. Both men went for their guns without hesitation. Porter fired too quickly. His horse reared at the unexpected sound; the bullet smashed wood behind him as Laredo fired at Wicker. Smoke blossomed in the tight area—Laredo fired three times as he moved to his right—and Wicker was down.

Someone else was firing. Hard sounds, orange flame vomiting from the smoke. Out of the corner of his eye Laredo saw Gus Porter shoved from the horse. Quinn Porter was in the doorway of the stable, a pistol in each hand. Laredo dropped to the ground to see under the smoke, firing twice at the man, seeing him jolted violently to crumple in the doorway.

Suddenly there was silence.

The smoke drifted away, and Laredo got to his feet. Pete Torres came from the right, a Winchester in his hands. "You all right?"

"I'm fine."

Porter's horse had galloped off. Gus was lying on his back, his shirtfront crimson. Wicker was dead, with three bullets in his chest. Laredo leaned against the hitchrack, punched out brass, and reloaded.

Pete went to the downed man in the stable doorway and pushed at him with the rifle muzzle, then shook his head.

It was over.

There was a telegraph a day's ride east, they told Laredo in the deadfall, the shack next to the stable. They gathered up the contents of pockets and saddlebags, left the deadfall owner five dollars to bury the three, and rode out.

Rufe Wicker had made many mistakes in his life, but in front of the stable he had made a really terrible one. But, as Pete said, he had been taking chances all his life. He had just not faced Laredo before.

About the Author

Arthur Moore is the author of fourteen westerns, including THE KID FROM RINCON, TRAIL OF THE GATLINGS, and THE STEEL BOX, published by Fawcett Books. He lives in Westlake Village, California.